PETER

PETER

Kate Walker

Houghton Mifflin Company
Boston   1993

Copyright © 1991 by Kate Walker
First American edition 1993
Originally published in Australia in 1991 by Omnibus
Books

Library of Congress Cataloging-in-Publication Data

Walker, Kate.
   Peter / Kate Walker. — 1st American ed.
      p.   cm.
   Summary: An ordinary fifteen-year-old Australian kid, who
enjoys riding his dirt bike and wants to be a photographer,
becomes confused about his sexuality when he finds he is
attracted to a gay friend of his older brother.
   ISBN 0-395-64722-3
   [1. Homosexuality — Fiction.   2. Australia — Fiction.]
I. Title.
PZ7.W15298Pe   1993   92-18948
[Fic] — dc20   CIP
                            AC

Printed in the United States of America

HAD   10   9   8   7   6   5   4   3   2   1

1

Friday morning! School holidays! Nine o'clock sharp! Mrs. Minslow arrived and went straight into her bull-dozer impersonation, rattling dishes and banging cup-board doors.

Sleep in? Forget it.

I held out for as long as I could by rolling over to face the wall and curling my pillow around my ears. But next minute — *Whaaaaaar!* My bedroom door flew open and my world was being sucked up the nozzle of a vacuum cleaner.

Mrs. Minslow is our cleaning lady-cum-semi-resident snoop. She never knocks, just barges straight in. You could be doing anything!

"Sleeping in at your age? I don't know what your mother's thinking of." Even with my eyes closed I wasn't spared the image of her floral stomach advancing on me. She sent her vacuum-cleaner nozzle on a seek-and-destroy mission under my bed. "Now, when I was a girl . . . !"

This nosy old jelly roll was once a *girl?* What a terrifying thought.

"And I'll need those sheets for the wash in five minutes, so up you get!"

I had my underpants on but I grabbed my clothes off

the chair and held them in front of me as I edged out the door. What a way to start the day — being perved on by a myopic old cleaning woman.

I got dressed in the bathroom and then went to get some breakfast. The state of the kitchen put me right off eating. Every cupboard door was open, and the contents of the fridge were spewed cross the breakfast bench. She'd been into everything.

It was too early to go to Tony's and bludge breakfast off him, so instead I went downstairs to the garage, pulled on my bike boots and helmet, and pushed my Yammi up the drive and on to the road.

The sky was white; the day was hot. Already it had the feel of an oven. And I'd been forced out into it, driven from my own home.

Go back and tell her to get nicked.

Right!

Pull the plug on her vacuum cleaner.

Good idea!

Drop your duds and flash her!

Yah!

They were all brilliant ideas. I did none of them. I walked my bike as far as Longworth Avenue, started it at the top of the hill, and rode it down into the subdivision.

2

A bit about me. My name's Peter Dawson, I'm fifteen, I hate my brother, and I'm not all that keen on my dad. He's only part-time now anyway, just wings in for Christmases, birthdays and crises. He and Mum have been divorced for a couple of years and I hope they stay that way.

Mum's a nurse in a doctor's surgery and she's great, you'd like her. She's the one who took me through the "birds and bees" routine when I was eleven. Of course I knew most of it already anyway, from dirty jokes and drawings on the back of toilet doors, but I liked the way she did it — straight from the hip. Know what I mean? Like I was a man and understood all the big words she was using.

My ambitions at the moment are to finish school, get my road license for the bike, and get a job with cameras: press photographer, television, movies maybe! And after that? I don't know, I haven't thought about it much. Make lots of money and be famous!

Anyway, to get back to the subdivision . . . My big payoff for getting up early was that I had the place to myself. I opened the bike up, gunned it down the straights, laid it through the corners and roared across the vacant blocks, raising dust behind me. (There's nothing built there yet, it's just pegged out, waiting for the real estate slump to finish.)

When I got bored tearing around the subdivision, I went on to the paddock at the far end. It's a little blind valley, and it's ours — that is, it's Dad's. He lets the boys ride there because they keep the scrub growth down and save him the cost of bringing in the slasher once a year to clear it.

The paddock is criss-crossed with bike tracks. In fact, there's hardly a landmark left that hasn't had a trail cut over it. Some of them are pretty hairy, like Muffler Hill. That's the one I went for. It's a slag-heap left over from an old mine, and I won't tell you how many times I've bombed out on it. You'll learn enough of my secrets without me baring the lot.

It's a steep climb, with a sharp turn at the top, so you can't afford to go tearing up it. But I like doing things slowly, taking my time and getting them right. Which is exactly what you *can't* do with the boys around. As far as they're concerned, unless you tear about like a suicidal maniac, risking paraplegia at every tree, then you're automatically a queer or a marshmallow or whatever the word of the week happens to be. Real men bust their skulls! Only pansies *practice!* Get the picture?

I came at the hill slow, with my gears low and my revs high. Passed the "muffler" at the bottom (that's a car exhaust jammed upright in the heart of a tree stump; the boys put it there). Hugged the shoulder of the track to keep clear of the rainwater ruts in the center. Didn't push it. This wasn't a race, it was just me. There was hardly any dust in the air and the only noise in the place was mine. And I like that.

I hit a patch of sand, dropped off the footpegs and

paddled through it. The bike wasn't going so well. It's only a 125 and it was pretty well flogged when I got it. And Muffler Hill is quite a haul, so I wasn't surprised the engine was surging a bit.

As soon as I felt the back tire grip again, I powered on. The rainwater ruts were edging me off into the weeds. I bounced across them to the other side. Kept moving, kept scanning ahead.

That's what I like about trail bikes: there's a thousand things to do, traps to watch for, decisions to make, all with split-second timing and no second tries. It's like space games, only better. It's real!

Rock steps coming up. No problem. I rapped the throttle and jerked the front wheel up and over the rise.

And the engine *missed*. I felt it through my boots on the pegs and my hands on the handgrips. One missed firing stroke in thousands, and it felt like a missed heart-beat. My nerves went on to super-scan waiting for it to happen again.

Second step. I rapped the throttle. The bike made the climb but it did it again — missed!

The worst place you can lose power is on a hill, and this hill was getting steeper. And if this rattling heap of chicken shit that tried to pass itself off as a bike was going to drop its guts on me, I wanted to know now!

I squeezed in the clutch and wrung the throttle for all it was worth. Really pressured the engine. It gagged and spluttered and died beneath my hands. I felt gravity tighten its arms around me, ready to bring me to a halt. I picked the best spot that was offering, laid the bike over on the slope and stepped off on the high side. And sat there, hanging on to the bike with one hand and hanging on to the hill with my backside. And swore.

If the boys turned up and caught me doing Spider-Man impersonations on the side of the hill, they'd rip me off something terrible. They'd never believe it was the bike's fault.

Fortunately, from where I was sitting I could see right across the subdivision, and there was no one in sight — yet. But they'd turn up soon. It was only a matter of time.

I'll spare you the tedious details of turning a bike on a cliff face and getting it down unpowered. Just take my word for it, it's a very classy maneuver. But it's also a *pig!*

—— 3 ——

I was down on the flat with my bike on its side-stand when the boys came in through the gate. Gaz was in the lead, with Rats and Jason and the rest straggling behind, about ten kids in all, mostly ones I knew from school. And because I was parked in the shade under one of the paddock's last surviving gum trees, they pulled in around me, hemming me in with exhaust fumes and noise.

"See your bike's not goin' again, Pete!" Jason said. He's a little toughie who rides an RX80, the smallest bike in the group.

"It just needs tunin', that's all," I said. I had the spark-plug out and wiped it down my jeans, leaving a long oily smear. "See?"

Jason gasped. "That's incredible!" and announced to the tree, "Peter Dawson's trick motorcycle will now roll over and play dead. Take it away, Pete!"

The boys laughed. So did I. You've got to be able to take a joke down here, otherwise you won't last ten seconds.

Gaz switched off his machine and sat back, holding it upright between his massive thighs. He's a big boy, our Gaz. Been shaving since he was thirteen; riding since he was ten. And because he'd been away for Christmas and had just got back, he asked, "What you fellers been up to?" He likes to think we can't do anything without him.

"Nothing much."

"Same old stuff, Gaz."

"Nothin' interestin', not since you were here last!" Jason said, and everyone groaned.

Jason's a crawler, but Gaz lapped it up. "No need to fight over me, fellers," he said, "there's enough of me to go around." And he unzipped his two-hundred-dollar leather jacket down to the waistband, letting his chest, covered with copper-red curls, shine through.

"*One* thing happened while ya were away." Rats grinned, and when the boys couldn't remember what it was, he curled his lip at them. "Friggin' dickheads! Can't yus remember what happened yesterday?"

The boys swore, and Rats laughed. He likes hassling people. That's his whole reason for existence — getting up people's noses.

"Come on, Rats," Gaz said. "Give! What happened?"

Rats smirked across the group and chanted, "Alice got an earring."

"Hey, yeah, Alice got an earring!"

7

The boys were ecstatic at being reminded.

"Alice got an earring."

"Come on, Alice, show Gaz ya earring. Don't be shy!"

Alice's real name is Eddy Peterson. I don't know how he got the nickname, probably no reason. He's in Year 10, same as me, but he's a baby — desperate to be liked. He'd do anything to be one of the boys. But he's definitely not the type you'd have tipped for a trail bike rider. He's got no coordination whatsoever, his legs and arms wobble when he's just *sitting* on a bike. The boys give him hell over it, but he keeps on turning up.

"Get 'is helmet off!" Rats yelled.

Eddy was already taking it off by himself, but a couple of pairs of hands shot out and dragged it off for him. He turned his head side-on to show Gaz his gold stud. Usually it's only the tough boys who get an earring; I don't know why Eddy thought he was going to get away with it.

"Has it worked yet, Alice? Got anyone interested yet?" the boys asked.

"It's the other ear that makes ya a faggot," Eddy said. "The right ear!"

"That's right, Alice, you got it in the right ear!" Rats called out. "What do ya reckon, Gaz? D'ya reckon Alice's joined the club?"

"Mmmmm." Gaz shook his head. "An earring in the right ear, Alice? Don't know about this one. Looks mighty sus, mighty sus."

The boys liked that. They took it up, tossed it around, made it their own: "Looks mighty sus, Alice! Mighty sus!"

"Might have to run him through the poofter test," Rats said.

That got them all yelling out ideas for what the test could be. Most of them were pretty off. Eddy played along with it, pretending to laugh, but all the while going more and more rubbery in the middle.

Gaz had the final say, naturally. He's a year or two older than most of the boys, and he just presumes he's the leader — therefore he is.

"There's only one thing that scares poofters more than big dicks," he said.

"What's that, Gaz?"

He kept the boys waiting, kept Eddy sweating. It's unusual for Gaz to join in when they pick on someone. He makes out he's above all that, like it's too childish. Maybe Eddy had been getting on his nerves, or he was bored that day and felt like doing something different.

He plumped out his pink cheeks and said with a smile, "Big hills, of course!"

I didn't get it. Jason and Clinton fell off their bikes and rolled on the ground, cackling. Most of the boys cracked up too. Eddy glanced around, grinning one minute, looking panicky the next, wondering whether he should laugh or not.

Gaz leaned toward him and said, real chummy, "Now, if you were to scoot up and down *there* a few times, Alice, we'd know you were all right. We'd know you were one of us." He let his gaze swing up the slope behind us, and Eddy's Adam's apple bounced in his throat.

I didn't blame it.

That part of the paddock is the only bit left untouched. It's a steep rise of thirty meters, sweeping up from the flat, where we were, to the back fences of the houses along Valley View Parade. (That's where I live;

you can see our roof from here.) The whole slope is covered with weeds and scrawny tea-trees hanging on by their toenails, and outcrops of rock that are near vertical in places.

It was all right for Gaz, sitting there on 850 cc's of shiny green Husqvarna; a bike like that can climb trees. But Eddy didn't pretend for a second he was going to try cutting a hill-climb on his low-powered Honda.

He blurted out, "We're not allowed up there!"

"Really?" Gaz leaned further forward, giving Eddy his full, undivided attention, all ninety-five kilos of it. "And why do you think that is?"

"We're not allowed near the fences! None of us are! You're not either!" Eddy said.

Bad move. That was not the line to use with Gaz. He settled his bulk slowly back on to his bike seat and said, "I ride where I like, feller. Got it?"

Naturally the other boys said the same.

Eddy was in trouble. His backbone must have felt like porridge; he was wobbling all over the place. It wouldn't look so bad if he was a little kid, but he's quite big. Everything about him's *loose*. Including his brain!

He called across the group to me, "We're not allowed up there, are we? You tell 'em, Pete, we're not allowed!"

My Adam's apple did a bounce then. I didn't want any part of this. It wasn't my problem.

I don't pick on Eddy. I'm not the least bit interested in giving anyone a hard time, and he's noticed it. He's even thanked me for it. "Thanks for not pickin' on me, Pete," he said once. "You're the only friend I've got in the paddock."

I'm not his friend. No one can afford to be friends with Eddy, he's too much of a dork.

I've got to be careful down here myself. I'm only just accepted by these kids as it is. Being in all "One" classes at school, and doing photography and coming top in English are considered highly unmasculine. I have to spit and swear and take an occasional leak against a tree to make up for it, otherwise I'd be considered sus too.

I was bobbed down beside my bike with the engine running, and that's right where I was staying — out of it! "I dunno," I said, and kept on fiddling with the carbi screws.

"No, you remember, Pete!" Eddy sat higher on his bike, trying to make eye contact. "We're not supposed to make a noise up near the houses. You remember?" He was pleading to be saved.

I shrugged. "Maybe there was somethin' said about it a while back."

"Ya do remember!" he told me. "Your old man said he'd kick us out if we made a noise." It was like he was blaming me now for what my old man had said.

Gaz's pale eyes slid across to me. "So your old man thinks he's gunna kick us out?"

I couldn't expect to shrug Gaz off so easily. "I wouldn't have a clue," I said. "He's not around any more . . . thank Christ."

"Then his mum'll do it!" Eddy yelled. "She'll kick us out!"

Gaz grinned. "Oh? Bit butch, is she? Lady wrestler? Weightlifter, maybe? Gunna toss us around, give us a thrill?"

"Yeah, go for it!"

"She into whips, Pete?"

"Yah, bondage!"

That was hard to take, having to listen to all the little

11

loonies cracking jokes about Mum. Especially when Eddy joined in: "Pete wouldn't go up there. He'd be too scared of his big butch mummy!"

"He'd better go up," Rats said. "If he don't, we'll all know why!"

As quick as that, *I* was in the hot seat! Everyone was glaring at me and suddenly *I* had to climb the rotten hill. This place is a minefield: one step and . . . *aaah!*

I glanced up the slope without really seeing it. "My bike'd make it up there," I said, "when it's going properly."

"Quit using your bike as an excuse."

"Can't use that one forever!"

"I'm not using it as an excuse!" I said. "I went up Muffler Hill this morning!"

"Who's never been up Muffler Hill?" Rats said.

Eddy hasn't, for one, and boy, was I tempted to say so, to swing the joke back on him. And I should have. It would have kept him from blurting out his next cretinous line. "I'll lend you mine, Petey!" he shrilled in a girlish voice.

The idiot! He thought he was being funny. He thought everyone was going to love him for playing the clown, when what he was really doing was handing out nails and wood so the boys could crucify him. And me along with him.

Straight away the boys started making cracks like: "What else've you two been lending each other over the holidays?" and "Check out his ears! See if he's got Alice's other earring!"

Then bloody Eddy did it again! "That's right," he said. "I gave 'im me other earring, the one for the right ear!"

"Ya gave me nothin', Eddy, so shut your face," I said. I was standing up now.

Eddy's mouth fell open.

"You've hurt his feelings, Petey. No more earrings for you."

"And he thought you were his friend."

"A lovers' tiff. They're having a lovers' tiff."

The joke had gone far enough. I rammed my screwdriver into the tool pouch at the back of the bike seat and zipped it shut.

"Not leaving already?" Gaz said. "We were hoping to hear more about your big holiday romance."

I swung my leg over my bike.

"Better go that way!" Rats nodded in the direction of the boulders and the tea-trees.

"Up ya go, Pete. Get it up!"

"Can 'e get it up, Alice? Is 'e any good?"

There was a war dance going on around me: mouths chanting, boots stomping. I tried to roll forward and found I had to work the throttle like crazy just to keep the bike firing. My on-the-spot tune-up had knackered it.

"Up you go, Petey."

I had to say something to save myself and swing the spotlight back on to him. I said: "Ladies first, Alice. After you!" It wasn't particularly clever and I felt lousy doing it. His eyes bugged out. I'd never called him Alice before and I guess he hadn't expected it.

But he surprised me more than I surprised him! He suddenly let fly at me with a long list of foul names, everything the boys had ever called him over the past months. Talk about recycling your garbage! It made me look worse still. I couldn't let him get away with it. I had to slam him.

"Go wank off somewhere else, cretin!" I told him. I got my bike moving, and puttered off and left him.

There's no masked avengers in the paddock, no one saves anyone else. If Eddy wanted to keep on riding here, he had to be able to handle it on his own.

"Peter, is that you?"

Damn! Mrs. Minslow. I'd forgotten she was there. She was in the kitchen, head in the fridge, rattling the shelves.

"Yes, its me." I kept on heading down the hallway.

"Have you been out on that bike again?"

"Yes, Mrs. Minslow."

"You'll kill your mother one day, the way you ride that bike."

"Only if she's standing in the driveway when I come in."

"What was that?"

"Nothing, Mrs. Minslow."

"Peter! On your way through, bring me the Ziff cleaner from the bathroom."

Because *she's* working, she thinks everyone else should be.

I deposited the Ziff on the breakfast bench, which was still smothered with jars and bit of food, and I kept on going.

"Peter?" Mrs. Minslow was out of the fridge now,

wiping her hands on her floral apron. "You're pale,"
she said.

"No, I'm not."

"Yes you are, my boy!"

"I'm not!" *And I'm not your boy.*

"Let me feel you." She came rolling toward me.

I backed away and opened a cupboard door between
us. "I'm fine!"

She stopped and stared, frisking me with her eyes.
"Have you fallen off your bike again?" she said.

"No."

Vince chose that moment to make his entrance. He's
my older brother, and he was wearing good jeans and
cover-up goo on his pimples, so he was obviously on his
way out. He broke the end off a wedge of cheese sitting
out on the bench.

"Come off your bike again, Ace?" he asked.

"No!"

"Look, Ace, why not forget all this kid stuff with the
busted elbows, and scraped knees, and go for the big
one — *brain damage!* Try it without the helmet, hey, and
make us proud of you!"

"Lord spare us!" Mrs. Minslow cried.

"Just giving the kid a little pep talk, Mrs. Min," Vince
said. "Spurring him on to greater things."

But it was his head she was gawking at. Vince had
forgotten there was one person yet to be stunned by his
new haircut. He started patting it.

"What on earth possessed your mother to let you do
that to your hair?" she asked.

She should talk; her hair's blue!

"Mum didn't *let* me," Vince said. "I did it myself."
It's the truth. He cadged twenty dollars off Mum,

15

saying he wanted his hair trimmed before he went back to uni next month. Then he went to a trendy hairdresser in town, and came home looking like a toothbrush. Short back and sides and long on top, which doesn't really work on him 'cause his hair is curly.

"Do you like his new perm?" I said. "He got it permed while he was at the hairdresser's too."

Mrs. Minslow huffed at me like I'd said something immoral. "Of course he didn't get it permed."

Sometimes I think I'm the only person in this house with a sense of humor.

Vince took a swig of orange juice from a plastic bottle and said, "See ya later."

"Where are you going?" Mrs. Minslow asked him.

"Out," he said.

"If your mother phones and wants to know where you are, I'd like to be able to tell her." She shuffled after him as he headed for the door.

"You can tell her," Vince called from the hallway, "I've gone *out!*" And the front door banged.

I broke off a piece of cheese for my breakfast too.

"Peter, do you know where your brother's going?" Mrs. Minslow asked me. The housework is just a front to her; she thinks Mum's really paying her to keep tabs on us.

"No," I said, "and I don't care."

She gasped and made out like I'd shocked her to her corn-pads. "That's a terrible thing to say. You *should* care about your brother. You should *love* your brother."

Good one, Mrs. Min!

Who'd have thought the old girl had it in her to crack a funny?

I nearly choked on my cheese.

5

Mum came home at 3:30, an hour later than usual. I was in the garage fiddling with my bike when she drove in. Vince bounded down the stairs and yanked her car door open for her.

"Madame!" He bowed like a butler.

Mum stayed in her seat and pushed her hair back, showing her gray roots. "How come your father gets the car with the air-conditioning," she sighed, "and I get this sweat-box?"

"He needs it for his self-image," Vince said. "You don't. You're cool."

"Oh?" She raised one eyebrow. "And what do you want?"

"Do I always have to want something?"

The eyebrow slumped. "Sorry, honey." (She calls us "honey" and things like that all the time.)

"Well, now that you're home," he said. "I wouldn't mind borrowing the car."

"Sorry, I haven't finished the shopping yet. I didn't get away from the surgery till late."

Vince's hand closed into a fist on the top of the door. "That's OK!" he said. He reached in and plucked the keys out of the ignition. "I'll get the stuff out of the back for you."

The hatchback was crammed with white plastic shopping bags. Mum has half a day off on Fridays and does all the shopping for the week on the way home. I came over to help too and the three of us marched up the stairs, single file, lugging the bags.

"New uniform looks nice, Mum," I said, from behind her.

Usually she wears all white to work — white dress, white stockings, white shoes — but today's uniform was blue.

"Thank you!" she said. "I like the color too. Would you believe Dr. Walkom suggested the change himself? Not like a man to notice what you're wearing."

"I noticed it straight away," Vince said. The stairs are narrow, and because he stopped, we had to stop as well. "It looks very nice, very sexy," he said. "Matches your eyes."

Her eyes are green, not blue.

"Don't let him con you, Mum," I whispered.

"I won't," she whispered back, then said, "Hike!" to get Vince moving.

We dumped our grocery bags on the kitchen bench and Vince tried again.

"Um, about the car, Mum. I promised David I'd take him in to Boss Brakes this afternoon to get re-lines for his brake shoes. He'll be waiting for me. He'll have taken them off by now."

"Like I said — sorry! I haven't bought the veggies yet."

"But I told him I'd be there!" Vince said. "I gave my word. And I know what you're like about people giving their word."

"You shouldn't have *given* your word till you knew you could get the car."

"Mum, he's driven me all over town. This is the first time he's asked *me* to drive *him* somewhere, and I don't want to let him down. We could last a day without veggies. You could buy them tomorrow."

"Why can't David last a day without his brake shoes?"

"You can't get them on the weekend," Vince said. "Boss Brakes is closed."

Mum frowned. "No. We agreed, when you got your license, that you could borrow the car any time so long as I didn't need it. I meet the repayments, I pay the registration, the car is mine." She pushed a frozen pizza at him. "And don't just stand there looking decorative in your new haircut. Put something away!" She pushed a juice bottle at me. "Oh, and Peter, I got a phone call at work today about bikes along the back fences. Is that right, were the boys riding up there?"

"Yeah." I busied myself sticking the juice in the fridge.

"You know they're not allowed up there, honey."

"It wasn't me," I said.

"You went out riding this morning," Vince said. "I was here when you came in."

He was shitty 'cause he couldn't get the car, so he was taking it out on me. That's usual.

"I didn't say I wasn't riding," I said. "I just said I wasn't riding the fences. What have you been up to that's making you go deaf?"

"That's enough," Mum said. She can't stand us fighting.

He's the one who starts it.

"Oh, touchy-touchy!" he said. "Did we hurt our little self when we fell off our bike?"

Mum squeezed a waistline into the loaf of bread she was holding. "Peter, did you have an accident today?"

"No, Mum."

"Are you sure?" She scanned me for telltale signs.

"I think if I'd wrapped myself around a tree, I'd remember it."

"Don't get smart." (Bike accident jokes are not *in* at our house.) "You promised to tell me if you ever had another accident."

"And I will! But I didn't!" (Laying a bike over on a hill is not an accident; I didn't have to tell her about that.) "Vince only said it to get you going."

"And I supposed that dirt on your backside just leaped up and hugged you," Vince said, "because of your magnetic personality?"

"Aw, get stuffed!" There was no dirt on my backside and I knew it.

"Don't you boys start!"

"I didn't start anything. I'm just standing here breathing. Or aren't I allowed to do that either?"

"Mum, where do you want this?" Vince asked. Slimy toad! Now he'd got her mad at me, he was going to grease up to her, making out like he was perfect and I was shit.

Vince and I used to be friends once, would you believe. When we were kids we just about lived in each other's pockets. We had special hide-outs, like Grandma's shed, and we'd prick our fingers and press the blood together, making ourselves blood-brothers like in the cowboy movies. (You wouldn't want kids doing that nowadays, would you?) And we had our own secret language with key words and hand signals so we could have conversations no one else was in on. We could send messages across rooms, or through walls even. Then Dad left and Vince saw his big chance to be the man of the house and walk all over me. So now we fight.

"Peter." Mum inhaled. "I want the truth. Did you or did you not have an accident?"

"No, I did not!" I said.

She didn't believe me. "Put that away." She pushed a jumbo box of laundry detergent at me. I went a short way down the hallway, then doubled back to listen at the door.

"*Did* he have a fall today?" she asked Vince.

"Probably. He wasn't gone long this morning and he's been grotty ever since he came back."

"Why didn't you phone me?"

"You don't like getting calls at work."

"This is different. If he's come off the bike, he could have been hurt."

"Mum, if he'd been hurt, the whole neighborhood would have known it. He's got a low pain threshold."

There was an angry rustle of plastic bags.

"If he's had a fall, the odds are he's hurt, and if he's hurt, I want to know about it. You're not a doctor, it's not for you to say, so in future — phone!"

"Mum, how much damage can he do to himself on a piddling little one-two-five?"

"The size of the bike makes no difference. *All* bikes are dangerous. You know what he did to himself last time, on this very same bike."

"He pulled his shoulder and sprained his wrist, that's all!"

"It was not a sprain! He fractured a scaphoid, and his handwriting's never been the same since."

"Mum!" Vince made it sound like a joke. (If it'd been *his* shoulder that got dislocated he wouldn't have thought it was so funny. I'm told it's about as painful as anything can get.) "You're not doing him any favors, you know, asking him every five minutes if he's hurt himself. Let him break a leg, it'll do him good. He's too soft."

"He is not soft."

"He is!"

"Your brother happens to be a sensitive young man . . ."

I am not "sensitive"!

". . . and I want him to stay that way."

"He's sensitive, all right. You can't look at him sideways these days without hurting his feelings."

"Then stop baiting him! At least he's *got* feelings to be hurt, which is a vast improvement on most males."

"I've got feelings too," Vince said. "I don't expect special treatment just because I've got feelings."

"You're not fifteen," Mum said. "It makes a difference."

"I was fifteen once and I was never like that."

"You were exactly like that."

"I was never a wimp."

"Your brother is not a wimp." She whispered it.

"He's going to be if you keep on coddling him, Mum. Let him go! Let him ride his bike. It's the only gutsy thing he does. Let him wipe himself out if he wants to."

"Oh, I see," Mum said, sounding calm, which is a bad sign with her. (Vince wasn't going to get the car if he stayed on this tack.) "So your advice is to let him hurt himself, let him turn himself into a scar-faced cripple, so long as it makes a man of him."

"Something had better," Vince mumbled.

Mum growled. "That's not being a *man*, it's being a moron. And it's not what I want for my son!"

"Yea, Mum!" I stepped back into the kitchen and gave her a round of applause.

"Oh, eavesdropping, very macho," Vince said.

"Peter!" Mum snapped at me. "I told you to put that box in the laundry!" And when I came back she was still cranky at me. "Will you please tell the boys to stay away from the fences?" she said. "I don't want any more phone calls at work."

"I won't be going down the paddock for a while," I said. "My bike's stuffed. I won't be seeing them."

"You could always *walk* down," she said.

I followed her into the pantry. "Mum, it won't make any difference what I tell the boys. They won't listen to me. They'll only do it more if I start laying down the law to them."

"I'm not asking you to lay down the law," she said. "Just remind them of their original agreement: that they can ride anywhere they like except near the fences. Surely you can do that?"

"Yeah, I could. And they could also take me apart," I said.

"They're your friends! What on earth would they do to you?"

"They'll think of something," I said. "And they're not my friends."

"You ride with them every day!"

"That doesn't make them my friends!"

Mum says Vince doesn't influence her, but he does.

23

He only had to pass the door with a "told you so" look on his face and she switched sides.

"I do everything else around here! Do I have to police the paddock as well?" she said.

"It's Dad's paddock," I said. "Let him do it."

"He doesn't get the phone calls!"

"Give them his number," I said.

"Peter! The boys aren't going to hurt you!"

See, she thought I was a wimp!

"All right." I tramped out of the pantry. "OK. Forget it. Don't worry, I'll do it. And when I come home bleeding from multiple stab wounds, don't blame me."

And I hoped I bled all over the carpet and the stain never came out, and she was left to face it every day, the memory of what she'd done to me.

Vince dropped a jar to get her attention.

"Be careful!" she said.

"Sorry, Mum." He picked it up, all smiles. "But I've had an idea. What say *we* do the shopping for you? We can drop by The Markets on the way to Boss Brakes and buy the vegetables. And you get to stay home and put your feet up. Cool scheme?"

Mum pushed her hair back harder, exposing more gray strands. "Who's this *we?*" she said. "Not you and David?"

That was a laugh: the two super-cools, Vince and David, getting around The Markets squeezing tomatoes and comparing grapefruits.

"No, me and Peter," Vince said.

"But Peter doesn't want to go out."

Right on, Mum!

"Peter, you'd help with the shopping, wouldn't you?" Vince gave me a wink and sort of jerked his

24

hand like he was trying to tell me something via our old code. I didn't remember any of it.

Mum answered him before I got the chance anyway. "Thank you," she said, "but I'd rather do the shopping myself."

Vince balanced the jar on the edge of the cupboard. "Is it because you don't like David?" he said.

"What?"

"You've lent me the car every other time I've wanted it, but now I want it for David, you say no."

Mum's lipstick had worn off and she looked tired. "At the risk of repeating myself," she said, "I need the car to do the shopping. It has nothing to do with David. I think he's one of the nicest friends you've had. I've even forgiven him for being the inspiration behind that new haircut of yours."

Vince's hand shot up to defend his hair. "See, you don't like him."

"I do!"

"But you don't *need* the car, not if we do the shopping for you."

"I told you . . ."

"And what happened to that big spiel we got the other day about men learning to do their own cooking and ironing and the rest of it?" He was pulling out the big guns now.

Mum sighed. "I don't want to have to go out again in the morning and *re*-buy all the things you've got wrong."

"If we get it wrong, we live with it," Vince said.

"No, *you* don't live with it. *You* live with frozen piz-zas, I'm the one who eats mushy bean sprouts for the rest of the week."

Vince shifted his weight against the cupboard. "Is your getting the right stick of celery more important than our learning survival skills?"

"Survival skills" is one of Mum's phrases; he was using her own weapons against her. (You don't have to like Vince to admire him. He's studying Law at the university and he's going to be good at it. In ten years' time, when he's defending people, there's going to be crims walking around all over the place, scot-free.)

"It's not just vegetables we need," Mum said, still fighting. "There's dry cleaning to be picked up, and the videos to be returned. You boys don't know the half of what I do around here."

"We can get those too," Vince said.

"But will you get it right?" She was holding her forehead permanently now, like she was getting a headache.

"They say that's the hardest part of parenting," Vince said, "letting your kids make mistakes."

That did it. Mum closed her eyes, and he knew he'd won. He wins so often now he doesn't make a big deal of it.

"Here, sit down." He pulled out a stool for her. "Make yourself a cup of coffee when we've gone. Have a rest. You deserve it."

Wow, she must have been tired. She didn't even gag on the sugar coating. "I'm glad someone thinks so," she said.

Vince stretched up to look in the glass cupboard above the bench. "Are the dry-cleaning receipts up here?"

Mum never made it on to the stool. "No, they're in the bedroom," she said. "I'll get them." She dragged her feet out into the hallway.

Vince already had the car keys. He hadn't let go of

them since taking them from the ignition. He found the shopping list in Mum's bag, folded it twice, very neatly, and held it out toward me.

"What do I want it for?" I said.

"Do the shopping for me and I'll see what I can do about getting you out of playing the heavy in the paddock," he said.

I kept my arms folded and stayed leaning against the fridge. "How?"

"I'll talk to Mum for you."

"I've already done that."

"No you haven't. You whined for thirty seconds, then gave up."

Vince has the clearest, deepest, most honest green eyes you've ever seen. Every used car salesman should have a pair.

"But if I don't go down the paddock, I'll be a wimp," I said. "I'll be chickening out."

"Better to be chicken than dead," he said, suddenly, miraculously seeing it from my point of view. "You try telling that group of little neo-Nazis where they can and can't ride, and you'll end up in the morgue." He was right, of course. Vince knows these kids, he went to school with most of them. Or their brothers.

"So why didn't you back me up when I was trying to explain that to Mum?" I said.

"Jesus! I cop it for interfering in your life. I cop it for not interfering. Make up your bloody mind! What d'you want?"

"Nothin' from you. You only do what suits you."

"So do you. Everyone does." He prodded me with the shopping list. "Don't be a shit, do this for me. I need this one."

27

"You need everything," I said.

He grinned, showing all his perfectly orthodontured teeth. "You know what you're going to be eating for the rest of the week if *I* buy the veggies?"

At least he doesn't crawl.

Mum came back and he started pleading my case straight away.

"You know, Mum, it's not fair to expect Peter to police the paddock. Peer groups react badly to one of their members assuming an authority role."

Peer groups? Authority role? *Puke!*

"Well, it's nice to see you showing some concern for your brother," she said.

"I'm always concerned about him."

I snatched the shopping list off Vince. If Mum was going to be that much of a pushover, she deserved to be conned.

Vince pretended to beam at me. "Isn't he a good kid? Didn't I raise him well?"

"Mmmm . . . ?" Mum said.

And I said, "Let's go."

David Rutherford lives two blocks down from us on Valley View Parade. The whole front of his house is hidden by a mass of trees; if it wasn't for the driveway and the mailbox you wouldn't know anyone lived there.

Vince pulled into the drive and stopped just short of

David's car, which was parked in the garage. It had its rear wheels off and its brake-drums showing.

It's an E. H. Holden, in top condition: burnished mags, very little chrome, and David had just had it spray-painted two-tone gray — charcoal on the top, light gray on the bottom, with thin black speed-stripes blending the two together. Very nice. Very classy. Makes you think straight away: what's under the hood?

Vince bipped the horn, and through the windscreens of both cars I could see David at the other end of the garage, standing under a strip light at a work-bench. Whatever he was doing, he kept on doing it for another thirty seconds.

Vince drummed his fingers on the steering-wheel. "You watch," he said. "He'll wander down here in a minute like a snail on Valium and say, 'What kept you? Don't you know I'm in a hurry?' "

The fluoro tube blinked out and David's white Reeboks came down the side of the garage. He did walk pretty slowly. But then he's tall, so every step covered an awful lot of ground. He ducked under the roller door and came out into the sunshine, squinting. The overalls he was wearing swam on him, and even then they weren't long enough for his legs. His jeans poked out the bottom.

He came up to our car, bent over double and leaned on the windowsill next to Vince.

"Where have you been?" he asked. "Don't you know what time it is?" The wristwatch he flashed in Vince's face looked like a piece of space-research hardware. "I had the brake shoes off an hour ago."

"Mum didn't want to give me the car," Vince said. "I had to work on her to get it."

David didn't look impressed. "Boss Brakes closes at four-thirty."

"If we get moving, we'll make it," Vince said. "Correction: if *you* get moving, we'll make it."

David's older than Vince, about twenty, I think. He's got a young face, but there are lines around his eyes — at least, there are when he's being hassled.

He rubbed his chin and you could hear the whiskers rasp. He's got really dark hair and pale skin, and that's given him a permanent after-five shadow. "I doubt they'll have exchange shoes in stock for this model," he said. "We'll have to go back Monday."

"OK, if they haven't got them, we'll go back Monday," Vince said.

"But your mother takes the car to work on Mondays."

"If I need the car, I'll get it!" Vince said.

David glanced past him to me. "Is he always this smug?" he asked.

I didn't know David all that well. We'd said hello a few times when he'd dropped in to collect Vince, that's all. So I just shrugged.

"I'm here! I've got the car!" Vince said. "I'm going to town. Do you want to come or don't you?"

With Vince it's always ultimatums.

David lowered his head, thinking it over.

Mum was right about him being the inspiration behind Vince's haircut. His is the same — short back and sides and long on top, except much longer than Vince's. David's hair hangs right down to his eyes almost. *And*, I noticed this the first time I saw him, it's got one blond hair in it. Every hair on his head is dark except for this one gold hair in his bangs. It's got to be dyed, it couldn't be real. And it stands out a mile. You can't miss it, close up that is.

Vince started a countdown on him and David made his decision: "OK." He pushed away from the window-sill and went back into the garage. I climbed in the back seat, and when David came out again, he had the brake shoes wrapped in a rag and a rug over his arm. He draped the rug over the passenger seat, holding it down while he got in.

"God, you're an old woman, Rutherford!" Vince said.

David didn't bite. "I wouldn't want anyone getting in my car in dirty overalls," he said.

His overalls weren't dirty, but I was surprised to see him wear them into town. Every other time I'd seen him he'd been dressed in million-dollar jeans and designer shirts. You know the kind, with the labels on the out-side.

He fastened his seatbelt, raised his hand from the buckle and flicked Vince on the ear, saying, "Just drive, cabbie."

I plastered myself against the seat. No one touches Vince's body. It's sacred! Even Mum has to sneak up on him to give him a hug for his birthday.

You just kissed your brake shoes goodbye, feller, I thought. But Vince put the car into gear, reversed down the drive and merged with the traffic without saying a word. And David continued to live and breathe in the passenger seat beside him.

Unreal!

Then, for his second amazing trick, David turned around in his seat and started talking to me. I mean, he actually started a conversation with me, like I was a real person, and very few of Vince's friends have ever done that. Younger brothers are usually seen as equal to warts and hangnails; everyone hopes they'll drop off.

So what's your game? I thought. Was he paying Vince off for being late?

"How's your bike going?" he asked me.

"OK," I said. "Um . . . how's your car going?"

"Not so good," he said, kind of mopey. "The gearbox is on the way out."

"You and your gearbox," Vince mumbled.

"I'm worried about it!"

"Can't you worry in silence?"

Vince didn't want David talking to me, that was clear, and I wasn't so keen on the idea myself. No matter what you say to older blokes, they always look down their noses at you eventually.

David raved on about his gearbox, about the synchros being worn, and not being able to change down through second.

I made the standard in-depth responses: "Really? . . . Far out! . . . Bummer!"

He reckoned he'd taken the gearbox out a thousand times in the last six months and, just for the sake of something to say, I commented, "You must change gearboxes like other people change underwear." Vince fired death rays at me via the rearview mirror. How dare I talk to one of his mates about their underwear?

David thought it was funny, though. He laughed. Then he asked Vince, "Hey, did you ask Peter about the photographs for me?"

"No. I forgot," Vince said. Via another flash of the green eyes in the rearview mirror, he asked me now.

"David wanted to know if you'd take some pictures of his car for him."

So that's why he was being nice to me. He wanted a few free pics!

David turned around in his seat again. "Vince showed me some pictures you took of dirt bikes the other day. They're really good."

"Um . . . Thanks!" *Vince had shown him some of my photographs?*

"I'd like something like that of the car," he said, "while it's still in mint condition. You know, before some twit opens his door on it and chips the paint. I'll pay you, of course."

"It's all right, you don't have to pay me. I don't mind," I said.

"No, I'd rather pay. That's the way I do things."

I'd look like I was crawling if I made a big deal out of doing it for nothing, so I said, "Fine." He was probably only going to slip me five bucks anyway. That set him off again, talking about the hassles he'd had with the spray painter.

I'd said I'd take his photos! He didn't have to keep on talking to me!

We pulled off the highway and stopped in front of The Markets. Vince dropped two twenty-dollar bills over the back of his seat and said, "Pick you up in half an hour. On the other side of the road."

The money fluttered to the floor and I had to go scrounging for it. He could have handed it to me.

"Pick me up here," I said. "I don't wanna go lugging the stuff over there."

"It won't hurt you!"

33

"I'm not standing over there with bags full of cucumbers!" I could afford to argue; he'd be in the shit if I changed my mind.

"What's this about?" David asked.

"This is how he got the car," I said, "by conning me into doing the shopping for him. Mum hadn't finished it."

David said to Vince, kind of quiet, "I don't like you conning other people for me."

"He's not being conned," Vince said. "We've got a deal. And I'm on a bus stop, Ace. Move it!"

"Are you happy with the deal?" David asked me.

"Dunno," I said. "I haven't got my share of it yet."

"I wish you wouldn't do this," David mumbled in Vince's direction. *Did Vince interfere in his life too?*

"If it bothers you, *you* do the shopping," Vince said. He snatched the shopping list off me and held it out to David.

And David called his bluff! He took it. Not angrily. He just slid the note from Vince's fingers, opened the car door and stepped out. Off came the overalls and there was the designer wardrobe — an immaculate black T-shirt and acid wash jeans.

He was serious. When he dropped his overalls on the seat, he peeled a fifty-dollar bill from his wallet and dropped that on top of them. "That's for the brake shoes," he said.

A bus pulled up behind us and the driver blasted us with the horn.

David tapped on my window and beckoned to me to get out. I stared at the back of Vince's neck. *He's your mate, do something about him!*

The bus driver blasted us again.

34

Someone had to move, so I opened the door. David kind of helped me out and closed the door behind me. Nothing happened for a second. The traffic zipped by but we just stood there. Then Vince pulled away with a small screech of tires and the bus slid into the curb to take his place.

This was silly. I didn't know this bloke. I didn't want to go shopping with him.

"Do you wanna wait?" I said. "He'll probably do a lap of the block and come back for you."

"Serves him right if he does," David said.

With his long, slow strides, he loped over to the shopping cart bay at the front door of The Markets and started trying out carts, looking for one he was prepared to push. He made his choice, handed me back the shopping list and said, "Do you mind navigating? I prefer to drive."

The Markets is a big steel shed filled with fruit and veggies laid out on trays or in boxes. A radio plays the whole time, slightly off the station, and a little tractor runs around terrorizing old ladies and bringing in more and more stuff.

Our shopping list said "lettuce." We came to a bin full of them. I took one off the top, and David watched me lower it into his personally road-tested cart.

"You happy with that?" he asked.

"I dunno," I said. "How excited can you get about a lettuce?" They all looked the same to me: bunches of limp green rags.

He reached across and plucked another one from the bin. "How about this one?" It looked exactly the same as mine.

Terrific! Not only did I have to buy the stupid stuff, I had to be criticized while I was doing it! I tossed my reject lettuce back on to the pile.

We moved on to the watermelon bin, where David did exactly the same thing to me. I heaved one out of the bin, but before I got it anywhere near his precious cart, he'd wheeled it around to the other side and was leaning over the melons, rapping them with his knuckles.

All Vince's mates are weird, but this bloke took the prize. I looked around, ready to die if I saw anyone who knew me.

Knock-knock-knock! He kept on doing it.

"Um . . . anyone home?" I said.

He smiled at me. "Come and listen. You can hear the difference."

I didn't rush in.

"Listen! You're supposed to be able to tell a good watermelon by the sound it makes."

"When you find one that plays Pink Floyd," I said, "I'll have it."

My second weak joke for the day. He thought it was hilarious, but it didn't stop him from rapping on watermelons: *knock-knock-knock!* and smiling to himself. He was having a wonderful time.

An old lady stopped her cart next to us and stood there, nodding. "It's so nice to see brothers getting on well these days," she said, beaming at us through her facepowder.

Brothers? David's dark and I'm fair. He's so tall he hovers up near the ceiling somewhere; I'd be lucky to come up to his shoulder. His clothes are immaculate, everything he wears is brand new, whereas my grotty bike gear wouldn't even find a home in a Goodwill bin.

Brothers! People see what they want to see. But David winked at me: *Go along with it. Don't shatter her illusions.*

Maybe the illusion was his. Maybe he would have liked a younger brother to get around with, to show off in front of, that sort of thing. I wouldn't have minded that either. But I got Vince.

I figured that maybe David didn't have a grandmother either, because he was really nice to the old lady. He chose a watermelon for her and lifted it into her cart.

"And it's a pleasure to see young men with such nice manners," she said.

He made out like it embarrassed him, but I bet it didn't.

The next old duck we came across had him lifting pumpkins for her. He was polite to everyone, like it was a perfectly normal thing to do. Which was OK by me, but I thought we were never going to get out of there.

I had to get him away from the old ducks. "Give us a hand," I said, holding a fistful of carrots and struggling to tear a plastic bag off the dispenser.

I noticed the old *blokes* didn't go for him in such a big way. We were poring over a display of tomatoes when an old slag with a beetroot nose started eyeing us off. He was standing on the other side of the bin from us, bagging tomatoes with his spotty hand. We were trying to work out the difference between two lots of tomatoes with different price tags hanging over them. They looked the same to us.

I suppose David and I were crowding each other a bit. We were leaving room for anyone else who wanted to buy the things. And I admit it is unusual to see two young blokes shopping. But the old slag started grunting and smirking, and looking around to catch someone else's eye, to share his discovery with them: *got a couple of ripe fruits here!*

That irked me. I hoped David hadn't noticed, and to ease a bit of distance between us, I shifted my weight slowly to the other foot. As I moved, David moved with me. He brought the tomato he was holding nearer to me so I could study it close up, and at the same time he laid his arm across my shoulders.

Our faces were so close I could see the tiny points of stubble across his top lip and smell his hair gel. I kept on talking about the tomato, but from behind his bangs he winked at me. Then very casually he turned his head, looked up at the old bloke, and smiled. The man hurled his tomatoes back in the bin. No way was he going to eat the same stuff we did.

David grinned and slid his arm off my shoulder, I bagged some tomatoes, and he moved on. Neither of us said anything about it, or about the checkout chick either. But that was different, that was just David.

She would have been about sixteen — not too old for me if she'd bothered to notice my existence. But all she saw was David. She kept peeking at him from under her eyelashes the whole time she was serving the customer ahead of us. Then when it was our turn, and David lifted the watermelon on to the weighing machine for her, she went into a rush of thank-yous. You'd have thought no one had ever helped her with anything in her life. (Maybe they hadn't.) He lifted other things on to the scale for her too, the heavy bags.

It was the end of the day. Her hair was untidy and there was veggie grot on the front of her apron, but boy, did she sparkle. She keyed our veggies through with "dancing fingers," she knew all the prices, she moved with a kind of rhythm as she worked. She asked us which side of the bin we'd got our tomatoes from, trusting us to tell her they were the expensive ones. Correction: trusting *him*.

She rang off the total, I paid her the money, but she turned to David and gave him the change, counting it out coin by coin, pressing each one into his hand so she could touch him.

I reckon if he'd winked at her the way he'd winked at me from behind his hair, she'd have leapt the counter for him.

How do some blokes do it?

He wasn't what you'd call super good-looking. Well, maybe he was; I don't know, I can't tell with blokes. But the face wasn't perfect. Maybe it was the smile. He smiled lots. Or the eyes! He had big honey-colored eyes. I'd noticed them when we were getting intimate over the tomatoes, and in the car too. He had a habit of looking you right in the eye when he talked.

And of course the hair was immaculate. Every strand was cut just right, so that it swept up from the back of his neck until it was really long and soft on top. And the clothes! Well, there was no way I could compete with the clothes.

"Call again!" the girl said with a little compressed smile as we walked away.

39

I'd seriously consider having my shaggy hair cut if I thought it'd get girls looking at me like that. I'd even stop dagging around in my grotty bike clothes so often!

"Are you coming back?" I asked David, when we were a discreet distance from the checkouts.

He grinned and gave me my change. "I wonder if Vince is here yet," he said, looking up and down the road.

Aw, *mega-cool!* I made a mental note to try out that one too.

Vince picked us up outside the fruit barn, late and smiling. "No joy on the brake shoes," he said. "Couldn't get exchanges. You're grounded for the weekend."

"What!"

David disappointed me. He should have been knocking round with Vince long enough to know he'd pull that stunt — leave his brake shoes at Boss Brakes.

"We'll use my car this weekend!" Typical Vince, trying to pass it off as an act of supreme consideration.

David got in the front, slammed the door and didn't talk much for the rest of the drive home.

Mum raved about the veggies when we brought them in and I told her David had helped, so she invited him to come round for dinner later. He accepted, and didn't Vince get narky!

When he came back from driving David home (I know he only lives down the street, but Vince drove him home), he stopped by my room to issue his latest order.

"Don't make a nuisance of yourself around David, OK?"

I propped my hands under my head. "Funny, *he* didn't seem to think I was a nuisance," I said. "But he thought you were a prize-winning turd."

"I'm just telling you, cool it with him."

"You don't tell me what to do."

"Have some sense."

Vince thinks all the brains in this family were used up on him.

"Jealousy's a curse," I said.

"I'm doing you a favor, Ace."

"Good heavens, no!" I grabbed the sides of the bed. "Not another one!"

"OK, I'm doing *him* a favor. He doesn't need you hanging round him."

"Why?"

"He's gay."

"What?"

"Camp! A poof! Or hadn't you noticed?"

"That? Yeah, sure I noticed."

"Yeah, sure you did."

Gay! Hmmm, that put me off him a bit.

8

A dinner to remember! *Me* sitting opposite the very thing the boys in the paddock are always on about — a *poof*.

Now that it had been pointed out to me, I did notice poofy things about him. Like the way he used his knife and fork — with delicacy! He didn't clang his plate like we did, and he had a special way of lifting his glass, coming in on it sideways and kind of sweeping it up in one movement.

41

Mum noticed it too. "Do you play the piano, David?" she asked. "You have lovely hands."

He didn't play the piano and he didn't seem to mind her asking either. He said he used to play the clarinet in the school band, and that forced me to expand my picture of him: as a schoolkid. How had he got on? Did he get rubbished at school?

He was as friendly to me as he'd been in the car, or at The Markets — maybe a bit more formal with Mum there. We talked easily enough; we had no trouble looking each other in the eye. Maybe he thought I'd known about him all along. A couple of times he even winked at me across the table, friendly little winks when anything was said about vegetables. I figured it had to be a habit with him — winking — because if he'd been flirting with me he wouldn't have done it with Mum and Vince there.

Naturally he couldn't lean close to me over dinner like he'd done over the tomatoes. That kept troubling me. Had he done it purely to tick off the old bloke, or had it been an excuse to move in on me? Did he get a buzz out of touching me? He'd been pretty close, and he'd looked deep into my eyes.

I didn't mind him fancying me. Funny, even if it's a bloke, it's still nice to know you're desirable. So long as the bloke isn't a creep and he does his adoring from a distance!

David wasn't a creep. He was nice. Ordinary. And that was my biggest problem, lining up those two images of him: being ordinary and being gay.

Sitting across the table from me, he looked pretty average — I mean straight. His shoulders inside his shirt were wide, and his forearms were covered with glossy black hair. All classic masculine stuff. He didn't

42

flap his hands or talk like a girl. Maybe Vince was lying! It was a possibility.

But then he'd do something like flutter his eyelashes (they were black and shiny too), and I'd *know* he was gay, and this other picture of him would come flashing into my head: the poof! the queer! doing it with other blokes! And every time it happened, I'd have to fill my mouth with curried tuna and stare at my plate.

Why would he do it? It wasn't like he couldn't score with the chicks. *How* could he do it? What made him want to?

He wasn't the first gay I'd come across (we've got a couple of highly possibles in Year 12 at school), but he was the first I'd had a chance to study close up, and frankly it wasn't easy to sit across the table from him and make conversation and think these things. I've got a pretty vivid imagination, and when an idea pops into my head, I see it all: wide-screen, technicolor, high-speed zoom.

David wasn't a mechanic either, like I'd first thought. (I should have known Vince was too much of a snob to be friends with a mere mechanic.) He was doing engineering at the university. His father was an engineer and his mother was a chemist.

"An *industrial* chemist," he said, "not a pharmacist. The old lady next door can't quite grasp the difference. She keeps asking Mum to bring home aspirin for her."

He talked a lot about his parents. Obviously he was living at home, happily. *Maybe his parents didn't know!*

". . . And when she found out Dad was an engineer," he said, telling us another story about the lady next door, "she offered him five dollars to fix her lawnmower."

His father was a consultant with Qantas.

I got the joke and laughed, and told myself firmly: He's an all-right bloke, get off his case! What he chooses to do in the back seat of his own car is his affair! And having said that, my brain was off again, zooming round the room, making movies.

Dinner was exhausting. I was glad when it was over. We carried our plates to the kitchen, David too. Vince rinsed them and I stacked them in the dishwasher. Then Vince spirited David away to the back room to show him something on the computer and I thought I'd better alert Mum to the possibility of live AIDS viruses rushing around on David's plate. I wasn't dobbing him in, I just thought it was the sort of thing Mum should know. I approached the subject as subtly as I knew how.

"Um . . . did you know David Rutherford was queer?" Naturally, I kept my voice down.

Mum closed the dishwasher door without diving for the antiseptic. "No, honey," she said, "I didn't know he was queer, but I did know he was gay."

Point taken.

"Um . . ." *Now for the question of the century.* "Is Vince gay?"

"Just because someone has a gay friend, that doesn't automatically mean *they're* gay, and I'm surprised at you for drawing the inference."

"I wasn't drawing the inference," I said. "I was just asking."

"Well, the best person to ask, I should think, would be Vince," she said.

Sometimes I wish Mum'd drop all the parenting crap and just be a parent: *tell* us things, hold our hands. I mean, it's confusing. What was she saying here? *I don't know either, honey, but if you can find out, let me know!* Or: *Funny you should ask. There's something your brother's been meaning to tell you!*

While he was entertaining David in the back room didn't seem like the right moment to ask.

Was there ever going to be one?

With my bedroom door open I could hear Vince and David talking in the room down the hall, and making the computer blip. Unfortunately I couldn't hear what they were saying, just the low drone of their conversation. Pity, it would have been interesting to know what a gay bloke talked about. It wasn't going to be girls, was it?

Mum called out, asking if anyone wanted cheesecake. I said no. Vince said yes, and he went out to the kitchen to get some. I passed the back room on my way to the toilet and poked my head in to see what program they were running.

" 'Pac man'?" I said. I'd expected something a bit more mature.

David sat on the edge of the chair, both hands on the joystick, looking worried. He was getting gobbled up all over the place.

"I haven't played this much," he said.

"I can see that. There's a system to it, you know."

"Oh?" He got up out of the chair. "Show me!"

"Well . . ." The game had defaulted and started again on its own by the time I sat down in front of the monitor. "You can't just run all over the place," I said. "You've only got so much time before they get you." He sat on the other chair, a little bit behind and to one side of me. I explained the route I was taking as I ran my man through it. "When you come in from the right . . ."

Kids hang all over you when you play video games, so you get used to an audience, but this was different. I couldn't really see him, just his knees and this hazy impression of his dark hair and his face to one side of me.

This is what poofters do, they sneak up on little boys and get them from behind!

I didn't really think that. Actually, I did. The thought just ran through my head, OK? We're programmed that way.

"Of course, if you come in from the other side," I said, "you have to go along the top instead."

"Can you show me?" he asked, and leaned on the back of my chair.

I restarted the game and waited for his hand to slip forward and touch my shoulder.

My man came in from the left, and despite having the jitters, I gobbled all the dots and got through the maze without the munchers catching me. Then the maze blinked out.

"What's happening now?" David said. Obviously he'd never got that far.

My man came back on to the screen and so did the munchers, but not the maze.

"Now you gotta do it blindfolded," I said.

"What! How?" he laughed.

46

"You have to remember where everything was," I said. "If you've played it often enough, you remember where the corners are."

I ran my man along the lines of dots — up, right, down, left, never missed a turn.

"Hey, you're good! Really good!" he said.

Possibly I impressed him so much that he forgot about getting a free feel. His hand stayed on the back of my chair the whole time. So he wasn't permanently on the make, it wasn't a preoccupation with him like it'd been with me all night.

Vince came back with two pieces of cheesecake.

"Did you know your brother was a computer-game wizard?" David said.

"Yeah." Vince gave me a glassy stare.

"Better go before I give ya an inferiority complex," I said. "Cheesecake looks good. Any left?" I lifted my hands from the joystick, got up and walked away from a fabulous score.

I had to go to the toilet first. By now I was busting for a leak. Nervous tension!

David left at eleven. I heard him go down the hallway and say goodnight to Mum. Then he came back to my room to say goodnight to me. He put his hand on the doorframe, and as his face appeared, his expression changed, right on cue. Most people's do when they see my room for the first time. His eyes did a double take of the ceiling and one eyebrow went up, disappearing under his bangs.

He was more diplomatic than most people, though. His sole comment was: "And it doesn't give you nightmares?"

My room is painted dark, dark blue. Mum let us

47

choose our own colors when she had the house re-painted last, and this was my choice: blue like the bottom of the sea. The curtains look like seaweed (I made them myself in a Year 7 Textiles class), and I've got mobiles and wind-chimes and all kinds of things hanging from the ceiling.

"Sometimes I run into a mobile in the middle of the night," I said, "and give myself a scare. But I never have nightmares."

"Half your luck," he said, like he wasn't a hundred percent convinced. He gave me a parting wink. "See you later."

Not if Vince can help it, I thought.

10

He sat on the end of my bed. I was *in* bed, under the covers, in my pajamas.

He didn't seem to be there for any particular reason. We talked about lawnmowers. He looked at me really closely. In fact, sometimes he leaned right over me and looked in my eyes, and his hair brushed my forehead. It was soft and tickly.

Other times the bed was really long and he was microscopically far away at the other end, and I couldn't understand a word he was saying. Or figure out why the hell he was there. And what was the big deal about mowing the lawn? He didn't have a lawn, for Chrissake, the whole front of his house was trees.

It's true, I don't have nightmares, but I do dream a lot. Not usually about blokes who sit on my bed and brush my forehead with their bangs. That was a first, and I knew where it came from — cheesecake at midnight.

Vince was in the kitchen when I got up. He was sitting at the breakfast bench reading the newspaper and drinking coffee, just in his pajama pants. They were hanging off his hips.

Mum was sleeping in. It's everyone for himself at our place Saturday mornings. I poured myself a glass of milk and broke into the muesli bars. Vince didn't acknowledge my existence, and that helped me dislike him sufficiently to ask the big question.

"Are you knocking round with David 'cause you're gay too?"

"If I was gay, Ace," he said without lifting his eyes from the editorial, "you'd be the first to know. I'd sneak into your room one night and scare the shit out of you."

"Yeah? And you'd end up on the floor," I said. He still hadn't answered my question and I figured that if I had to live in the same house as him, I had a right to know. "So why ya hanging round with him?"

He slurped his coffee, scratched his armpit, and under cover of rattling the newspaper, mumbled, "I like him."

"Is that it?"

"He's a decent bloke."

"It's gunna look odd," I said. "You know what everyone's gunna think. You're gunna get yourself talked about."

Vince shrugged, and all the small muscles across his chest moved. "That's better than not being talked about," he smiled. Even though he was reading the paper, he seemed willing enough to talk, so I kept asking questions.

"What's he like at uni?"

"Brilliant," he said. "You've got no idea how many dummies there are in that place."

"Um . . . what's he like with the other blokes?"

"You mean does he ponce around the corridors picking up the boys?"

That's sort of what I'd meant, roughly. I nodded. "Yeah."

"Well, he's not the campus faggot, but he's certainly had his flings."

"It doesn't bother ya?"

"Why should it? It's his dick, he can stick it where he likes." He turned the page but kept on talking. "He's had to dip out of the camp scene for the present, though. Old boyfriend problems. The guy doesn't want to let go."

"Does he talk about that kind of stuff with you, boyfriends and that?"

"Sometimes. Do your mates talk about girls?"

Tony doesn't talk about anything else!

"What sort of things does he tell ya?"

"Things he doesn't expect me to blab to everyone else!"

We haven't talked for years, this could have been a rare moment. He *would* clam up just when the conversation got interesting.

"So what's in it for him," I said, "knockin' round with you?"

"Nothing. We go out sometimes. He drives me home

50

when we finish lectures together. There doesn't have to be anything in it."

"You're running a risk. You might get bashed if people think you're queer."

"I might."

He thinks he's so cool!

"Has David ever been bashed?"

"None of your business, Ace. And I'm trying to read the paper!"

Not being brilliant or exotic or even interesting, I couldn't expect to hold his attention for long. So I told him where he could shove his newspaper, *sideways!* and took my muesli bar elsewhere.

—— 11 ——

Tony came round on Saturday morning. He leaped into my room, ringing the wind-chimes and setting everything in motion. He's short and energetic and tends to ricochet around the place.

"I got it!" he whispered, loud enough for the next-door neighbors to hear.

"Got what?"

"*It*, dummy, *It!*" Tony's Italian, and he gets emotional very easily. "See — *it!*" He dug a 35-millimeter film container out of his shorts pocket and threw it to me.

"Oh, it," I said, a bit flat. "So you really did it?"

"Of course I did. I said I would! Don't I always do what I say?"

"Yeah! Sometimes."

He sat on my desk, hunched forward with his feet on the chair. "Run that through the magic potions, Mr. Kodak, and see what comes out. Or d'you want me to tell ya?" His eyebrows did high jumps. He was going to tell me anyway.

"Ya should have been there. I got her sunbaking *full* front and *full* back, and rubbing suntan lotion on herself, and doing the backstroke across the pool. It was cosmic!" He pulled three thousand different expressions of ecstasy in three seconds. "Ya should have come. There was room in the tree for both of us!"

"Mmm," I said. "Did anyone see ya?"

"Nah, only Sophie."

"Your sister? Shit!"

"She's all right. She won't blab. Sophie's cool."

"Geez, Tony, what'd she say?"

"Nothing. Just that I was a disgusting pervert."

"Did she see my camera?"

"I don't know. What's it matter?"

"If she saw it, she'd know it was mine."

"She doesn't know your camera."

"But if she saw it she'd know it wasn't yours, and if it wasn't yours, she'd know it was mine."

"So? . . . Aw, I get it, I see, you don't want Soph thinking you're a disgusting pervert too."

"It's not that, Tony."

"Yes it is. I know. I understand!" He slapped his hands to his chest. "Who's gunna understand better than me that a bloke's gotta protect his image in front of the chicks?"

"It's not that, Tony!"

"It is!"

"OK!" I admitted it.

"So when you gunna develop 'em?"

"Not now. Not with Vince snooping around."

"Doesn't matter," Tony said. "We haven't got time this mornin' anyway. We're expected down the Mall." He leaned back, fingering one of the wind-chimes with a rare bit of gentleness. "Guess what I've got?"

"Brain damage?" I said.

"Eat ya heart out, flunky. I've got a date with Gloria Jansen." I burst out laughing.

"Aw, shut up, Dawson, you'd die for a date with her."

"I'd die if I got one. She's plastic."

"Spastic?"

"No, plastic. It's worse."

"Look, mate, anyone who doesn't want a date with Gloria Jansen needs his head read. Or his hormones counted. She's just so . . ." He sucked air through his teeth.

"I hate to tell you this, Tony, but the whole world isn't like you. Not everyone goes for that sort of chick."

"Only because they know they couldn't handle her. Whereas me . . . !"

Tony and I have been friends since Year 5 and he's always been like this: sex-mad and up himself. But he's never boring, you've got to give him that.

"There'll be someone there for you too," he said. "I arranged it."

"Who?"

"Come along and find out," he smirked.

"Tell me first, or I'm not coming."

53

"You'll come," he said. He knows me pretty well.

"If you won't tell me her name, she must be a dog."

"Would I fix you up with a dog?"

"You'd do any bloody thing, Tony."

"Maybe for a joke, but I'm not jokin' this time. She's a nice chick. Take my word for it."

"Who is it, then?"

"Can't tell. I'm sworn to secrecy."

"What's her initials?" It was important to find out: Tony knows some pretty weird girls.

"Burning matches under the fingernails won't get it out of me!" he said.

Maybe not, but I knew what would. I took his film out of the container, held the cartridge in one hand and the end of the celluloid strip in the other, and very slowly I started jerking it out, exposing the negative centimeter by centimeter. There's a long trace on a film, I wasn't really exposing it, but Tony didn't know that. He froze.

"You wouldn't!"

"Oh, wouldn't I? And her first initial . . . ? Tony! You bloody idiot, this is color film!"

"Of course it is! Who wants black-and-white tits?"

His pictures, if you haven't guessed already, were of a lady who lives behind him, and who skinny-dips in her pool and sunbakes nude behind a three-meter-high metal fence. But Tony happens to have a *six*-meter-high lilli-pilli tree in his back yard, and he just about lives in it now. Along with my telephoto lens.

"Tony, I can't develop color film! You need thousands of dollars' worth of gear for that. I told ya, I can only print black-and-white."

His jaw hit the carpet. "And after all I went through, hanging up in that bloody tree, getting bloody shit on!"

He started to spit as he talked, and I sat back, out of range. Tony doesn't handle disappointment at all well. He took back his film and cradled it in his hands like a dead bird, mooning over it. "Me good pictures!"

"You could take them down the Mall and get them developed there," I said. This is the way things usually go with Tony and me. He comes up with the hare-brained schemes, and I tell him how to make them work. "It'll cost you, though," I said. "Twenty-four exposures — eighteen dollars."

The word "exposures" brightened him up; it doesn't take much. His face came alive again. "That's only nine bucks each."

"Don't look at me, I'm broke," I said.

"You said you'd develop 'em for me."

"Develop 'em in my darkroom, yeah, not fork out nine bucks."

"It's still developing them!"

"This is big money you're talking here, Tony. I don't have nine bucks."

"If you gave up riding that friggin' bike for a while, you'd have it."

Tony hates the bike. It's the only thing I do without him and, to tell the truth, that's one of the reasons I took it up. We go to the same school, we're mostly in the same classes, we catch the same bus. I needed to do something without him. I wasn't trying to cut him out — he's a terrific friend — but I needed, I dunno, new experiences! With Tony it's always the same thing.

And I think he sort of guessed, because he goes on about the bike being "infantile," and about it being a substitute for sex.

"Give the sissy thing away and come down the Mall

and get some *real* action going!" he said. "You're gunna have to do it eventually. You can't put it off forever."

"Put what off?"

"*It*, mate. *It!*"

"I think we've had this conversation before," I said. *We've been having it since Year 5.*

"Admit it, you're interested," he said.

"Of course I'm interested."

"Well? *Do* it, before the bloody thing drops off in your hand."

"You've never done it!"

"I've got close, though! And let me tell you . . ."

A million times I've heard this story about his one near miss.

I jumped up. "I'll come if you promise not to tell me!" I said.

Tony leaped off the desk, stretched his face into a huge grin and pretended to rough me up. "Told ya you'd come," he said.

You can't help but like him, he's a crazy bastard.

12

At the Mall we found Gloria sitting in the Doughnut Shop, on a stool in the window, with her long legs wrapped around each other and the little tie things at the sides of her shorts dangling down.

Tony made grabs at the air. "Let me at it!"

We were on the other side of the walkway, with a

million shoppers streaming past in front of us. Gloria hadn't spotted us.

"You just gunna bowl up to her and start talking?" I said.

Tony grinned. "Yep!"

"What about?"

"Doesn't matter. Chicks don't care what you talk about so long as you make noises at them. They spend half their lives dreaming of blokes like us just breezing up and saying, 'Hi, doll!' I've got three sisters — I know!"

Having a brother has disadvantaged me in more ways than one.

I tried it out: *"Hi, doll! . . .* Tony?"

"Yeah?"

"It's not gunna work."

Tony sucked in his stomach, poked out his chest and lowered his eyelids — his Latin Lover pose. It looks pretty hilarious when he tries to walk that way. "Watch and learn, lover boy. Just do as I do, and watch and learn." He signaled for me to follow him.

A woman pushing a huge stroller was trying to get out of the Doughnut Shop as we were trying to get in. Tony hurdled the front of the stroller and bounded on, but I stood back and waited for her to maneuver the thing out, and she smiled at me.

She was pretty young to be a mum, and half way through the door her purse fell off the top of the sunshade thing over the kid's head, and I wondered, am I getting the come-on-here? You know, like the dropped handkerchief. I made a dive for the purse.

Personally, I wouldn't mind having it off with an older woman. I reckon it'd be a great way to learn.

She'd know everything and she could tell you what to do — not like a young chick, who's got as many clues as you've got and is just going to lie there.

But the woman pounced on her purse almost as fast as it fell to the floor, so it looked like a genuine drop. And I went back to having Tony for a teacher. Pity!

Tony was already leaning on the counter next to Gloria, yabbering away and waving his hands in the air. I tell him he does this, but he won't believe me.

Gloria's one of our Year 9 tartlets — young chicks who hang around the older boys and act sexy. Tony and I aren't officially "older" yet, but we will be when school starts again in a couple of weeks' time. And Gloria looked noticeably interested already. As he talked, she sipped her milkshake, tossed her frizzy red hair and blinked up into his face.

I also spotted the mystery "someone" for me. It was Sophie, Tony's younger sister. She was sitting against the wall, on a stool next to Gloria. I couldn't see her face but I knew her from the back, from the big loose top she was wearing. She wears them all the time — to hide her big boobs, Tony says. It works! I'd never noticed they were big till he pointed them out to me.

Sophie is definitely not a tartlet, and I was surprised to see her knocking round with Gloria. Some people get desperate for friends over the holidays, that might have been it.

Sophie's nice. She does well at school, and she's a great artist. One of her art projects is hanging in the library. It's a collage of famous Renaissance paintings, mostly pictures of round-faced angels and Madonnas with flowing hair, which is what *she* looks like, oddly enough — very Italian; pretty; a bit sorrowful looking.

She's got beautiful hair, and she doesn't do weird things to it either, just clips it back or, like today, lets it hang loose across her shoulders. And her lips are a natural deep maroon color. I wish she wasn't so quiet, it makes her that bit harder to talk to — not that we've ever really talked. I don't know her all that well, because whenever I've seen her, Tony's always been around.

The shop was full of parents with kids and shopping bags, and it took me a while to fight a path through them. When I finally got there, Tony was well into his spiel. "You gotta come and see it. It's really something!" he was saying.

Gloria shook her head and sighed, "Really?"

Tony had let his stomach out by this time, but he was still giving her his "drooping eyelids" look. Probably because her top was gaping and from where he stood he could see down the front of it. It was a loose singlet thing that clung to the shape of her breasts.

"Tell us more," Gloria giggled.

"Don't encourage him," Sophie said from behind her hair. "You'll never get rid of him."

"Peter's here, Sophie," Tony said, forcing her to talk to me. She mumbled, "Hello," I muttered, "Hi," she leaned back over her milkshake: end of conversation. *Great stuff, Tony!*

"I've been telling the girls about your darkroom," Tony said. "They wanna come and see it. So tell 'em about it!" He gestured to me like I was supposed to go into a tap-dance.

"Well," I pushed my hands into my pockets, "it's not that big. We've got a black-and-white enlarger . . ." I don't get nervous talking to girls, it's just that if I'd had to strike up a conversation on the spot like that, I'd have picked a better topic than darkrooms. "It can do enlargements up to this big." I held my hands out a few centimeters wider than the actual size.

Gloria turned on her stool, leaned back on the counter, and stared at me out of eyes ringed with thick black lines.

Will someone tell me why girls draw black rings around their eyes? What is it I don't know?

Her eyelids just about creaked under the mass of eyeshadow, and her lipstick was a solid bank of purple. The one thing I liked about her, her big pale freckles, she'd blanked out with make-up.

"Well, if it isn't the famous Peter Mark Dawson!" she said.

I put my hands back in my pockets. "I didn't know I was famous." And how did she know my second name? Tony!

"Oh gosh, and he's modest too!" Gloria performed a little belly dance on the stool in front of me. She's got a good figure, but she's always flashing it. She's the kind of chick who has no secrets left, if you know what I mean. Not the sort I go for, but she seemed to be going for me. She slumped forward so her top gaped in my direction.

Tony came sliding along the counter, taking up a new droopy-eyed position to perv from. "So, you girls coming?" he asked.

Gloria screwed her purple mouth to one side. "Dunno. What about you, Soph, you wanna go?"

"I did photography as an interest elective last year," Sophie said. "I've been in darkrooms before."

I was glad to see that being with Gloria hadn't

changed her. Sophie was still her usual low-key, sensible self. Gloria's a scatterbrain.

Gloria crossed her legs and tossed her hair and said, "I did sailboard riding last year. Ever been sailboard riding?"

The question was directed at me, so I answered, "Yeah, once."

"And did ya like it?"

"It was all right."

She lowered one shoulder. *"Just* all right?"

"Yeah," I said. "I prefer surfing."

"D'ya hear that, Soph? He *prefers* surfing. *Prefers* surfing."

I can't stand the way some people do that, rip you off over some perfectly normal thing you've said.

Sophie said, sensibly, "I thought you were a bike rider."

"Are you a bikie?" Gloria piped up.

"I didn't say he was a *bikie,*" Sophie said. "I said I thought he *rode* a bike. Riding a bike is not the same as being a bikie."

"That's true, it isn't," I said. *Thank you, Soph.*

"What kind of bike d'ya ride?" Gloria gave another wriggle.

"A Yamaha," I said. I didn't mention the engine size. "A dirt bike."

"Hey, when you girls come to see the darkroom, Pete can take you for a ride!" Tony said.

Suddenly my bike was acceptable! Because it could be useful to him.

Gloria swung her foot up and down, bringing it closer and closer to my leg — like within two centimeters of kicking me in the shin. I've watched her work this routine before: swinging her legs, tossing her hair and letting the older boys perv down the front of her sports shirt. And even though I didn't like her, it was nice to be the one getting the attention. Tony's going to hate me, I thought, but so what?

"Yeah, I'll take ya for a ride," I said.

That interested her. "Sophie, you wanna go for a ride on Peter's bike?"

Sophie said no, and Tony pounced on her. "Don't be silly, Soph, of course you do. It's fun!" *As if he'd know!* "You gotta do things. You can't just sit on your big fat butt all day."

Tony's always at her about being fat and having a big backside. He's got no idea of proportion; with boobs like hers, she'd look ridiculous with skinny hips — like an ice-cream cone. A double!

"She doesn't have to if she doesn't want to," I said. "Not everyone likes bikes."

"Thank you," she said.

"Any time," I replied.

"And do you wear leather and boots to make yourself look macho?" Gloria asked.

I knew what the doughnuts felt like having the middles knocked out of them.

"No, I don't wear leather," I said. "I don't even wear a jacket. I wear boots, though. You're an idiot if you don't wear boots. You're askin' to break an ankle." Bloody chick, now she had me defending myself. I dug around in my pockets. "You got any money, Tony? I feel like a drink."

Gloria slid her milkshake container along her leg toward me. "You can have a sip of mine."

I looked at the yellow froth clinging to the inside and asked, "What kind is it?"

"Banana," she said.

"Thanks, but I don't like banana milkshakes."

"I do!" Tony lurched forward, his tongue hanging out. She gave the container to him, but she kept on talking to me. "He doesn't want mine, Soph. He thinks I've got germs. Let him have yours. Aw, Soph, ya pig, you've drunk it all."

I found some change in my pocket and wandered off to buy a can of drink.

The girls left soon after that, with Gloria *ordering* us not to follow them.

"As if we would," I mumbled.

Tony slurped up the dregs of her milkshake. "Get your darkroom ready to roll, mate. She's comin'!"

"Ya gotta be jokin'," I said.

He looked at me as if I was stupid. "Of course she's comin'! She's dying to come!"

"She was ripping us off the whole time, Tony." Him too, or hadn't he noticed?

"That's just the way chicks act. They gotta, or we'll think they're sluts."

"I wouldn't think a girl was a slut just because she said something nice to me. 'Do you wear leather to make yourself look macho?' What a put-down!"

"Forget it. It's Soph you want anyway. Leave Gloria to me. Did ya see her give me the come-on, then try an' make me jealous?"

"Is that what it was?" I laughed.

"Christ. Dawson, don't you know anything about chicks?"

"Apparently not."

"She'll come, mate. You'll see."

"Wanna bet?"

"Yeah!"

"Nine bucks?"

"Yeah!"

"You're on!"

—— 13 ——

On the way home I told Tony about David.

"We had a poof for dinner last night."

"Taste any good?"

"Dunno, I didn't have any."

"I should hope not! Where'd he come from? Is your Mum goin' out with him?"

"No, he's a friend of Vince's."

"Is Vince a poof?"

"I don't think so."

"D'ya ask him?"

"Yeah. He said he wasn't."

"And you believe it?"

"Who knows with Vince?"

"Maybe he's trying it on," Tony said.

"He's had girlfriends . . . well, *a* girlfriend. I dunno, I reckon he'd hang around with gays just to make himself look exotic."

"Or he could be *bi*!" Tony said. "Your brother's weird enough to be anything."

"The camp guy wasn't weird."

"Come off it!"

"Dead-set, he was OK. He lives on our street — drives the E. H. Holden. You know, the bloke with the spiffy haircut?"

Then I thought maybe I shouldn't have told. *Too late now.*

"Him?" Tony said.

"Yeah."

"*Him!* Shit, you wouldn't have picked it."

"You would close up."

"Why? What'd he do?"

"Well, he does things with his hands that are a bit . . ."

"Did he grope ya?"

"Tony! Not everyone's a sex maniac like you. No, his hands are sort of . . ." — I tried to give a demonstration — ". . . graceful! And he dresses up a bit. And he's got this one blond hair in his bangs which is really noticeable. It's gotta be dyed!"

"Did he put the hard word on ya?"

"Tony! He came for dinner!"

"So?"

"Mum was there! Vince was there! What was he gunna do?"

"He might've done anything. You're taking your life in your hands. You could've got AIDS."

"You can't get AIDS from having dinner with someone."

"How do you know?"

I gave him the spiel from Mum's latest brochure. She's always bringing them home from the surgery.

"But I had a dream about him," I said.

"The camp bloke?"

"Yeah, last night. I dreamed he came into my room and sat on my bed."

"And!" Tony's eyes got wider. Wider than usual.

"He talked about lawnmowers."

"*And!*"

"That's it, he just talked."

Actually, it hadn't been a dream, not *totally*. It was one of those half awake ones where I knew what was going on so I let it run, just to see what would happen. We're all curious. Even Tony was disappointed when the best I had to report was getting my forehead brushed with his bangs.

"You ever dreamed about a bloke?" I asked him.

"No!" Tony's eyebrows went dead flat. "Never!"

With a denial like that, maybe he had, but he sure as hell wasn't talking about it.

—— 14 ——

Monday morning the first bikes arrived in the paddock at 10:14 A.M. I was lying on my bed, fully dressed except for my boots, watching the numbers on my digital clock change over.

10:27. The first bike started up the hill. I knew whose it was by the sounds it made — Clinton's Honda. It's geared low and has a scream like a chainsaw. He made it to the top, changed down and roared along the fences. I pulled a *Two Wheels* magazine from under my bed and propped it open on my chest. It was one I'd read before, so I just looked at the pictures.

A second bike started up the climb — Rats's Kwaka — and Vince appeared in my doorway.

"That's our cue, Tonto. Let's go lean on the bikies," he said.

I let the magazine fall on my face. "Piss off, I'm meditating."

"Don't be like that, Ace. I tried. I had Mum ready to go down there and face them for you herself, single-handed! But then she called Dad about it and you know what he's like. 'A man's gotta be a man. He's gotta do his duty!' "

"Yeah, like you do for yourself."

"I tried, Ace!"

"I bet ya did!"

"Look, I said I'd go down with you."

"Since when did I need you to hold my hand?"

"Let's go. I've got other things to do."

"I'll go when I'm ready, fart-arse."

"You can't be helped, can you?"

"I don't need your help."

"You stupid little twit. I don't know why I bother with you!"

"Don't bother! Nobody asked ya to! I don't need it! You're not my old man!"

"You're developing a really massive problem about that!"

"When are ya gunna drop dead?" I said.

"And when are you going to grow up?"

"Piss off!"

He shrugged and left.

The bikes beyond the fences started churning up the

dust, which drifted in through the flyscreen along with exhaust fumes. With all the noise they were making, they might as well have been in the bedroom with me. I waited a few minutes, then padded down the hall in my football socks.

Face-ache was in the kitchen, mixing breakfast cereal and strawberry ice cream together. (If the artificial flavorings didn't get him, I hoped the preservatives would.) He recited the "Ode to Remembrance" to me as I went down the stairs: *"They went with songs to the battle. They were young, straight of limb, clear of something* or other. *They fell with their faces to the foe."*

I pulled on my helmet and that blocked him out. If only it was always so easy.

I started my bike and it just about shook itself to pieces on its side-stand. I couldn't take it down to the paddock like that. Might as well go down naked with butcher-shop diagrams inked on my body, showing the boys where to slice me up! I killed the engine and hung my helmet over the handlebar.

Face-ache was still up there, reciting: *"They shall grow not old . . ."* I ran the bike up the drive.

I had a back-up plan. Out in the sunshine, I walked the bike past David's place. His garage door was open and his car was still inside, still on blocks. Vince hadn't managed to get Mum's car, either, like he'd promised. Maybe Boofhead was losing his touch.

One thing was sure, he was going to lose his cool when he found out I'd been to see his bestest buddy without him.

15

I peeked inside the garage first. There were paint tins lined up in front of fuel tins lined up in front of garden tools all along the walls. A place for everything . . . but no David.

I couldn't spot a door anywhere in the jungle across the front of the house, so instead I went down a path that ran alongside the garage. I don't usually like going round the backs of people's houses. You don't know what they might be doing. Sunbaking! Skinny-dipping!

Not that I had much chance of sneaking up on them; the pathway was gravel and crunched under my boots. Someone had just hosed the place, and the huge tree-ferns drooping over the path dripped water on me. The ground smelled mossy.

Then the path hooked right and there, in a kind of alcove, surrounded by plants in pots, was their long-lost front door. Only their milkman knows! I thought.

The door was open but the security screen was closed, and from where I stood I could see through its bronze mesh. A cream telephone sat on a glass table beside a stand of tall, exotic-looking reed things in a pottery vase. Very "decorator"!

A doorbell glowed on the door-frame, but I didn't

press it. I hate doorbells, they either buzz too loud or play stupid tunes. Anyway, a woman passed by the door, reading a book and eating an apple. I thought she hadn't seen me, because she kept on going, so I hung back. Maybe I should skip, I thought. Maybe getting up Vince's nose wasn't worth it. This could start a war. Or maybe David would think I was bludging favors, and tell me to get nicked!

The woman stopped, leaned back, and peered out through the security screen. "Hello?" she said. And gosh, she was pretty.

I stood up straight. "Mrs. Rutherford?" I asked.

"Yes?" She came up to the door.

Perhaps *this* was Vince's motive for knocking round with David. His mum was a honey. She had a face like a young girl's: a little pointed chin and big bright eyes. Her hair was cut short and spiffy like David's, and her earrings were big Aztec coins that hugged the sides of her face.

And I had to make conversation with her!

"Um . . . is David home?" I asked.

"Yes, but he's getting ready to go out," she said. "What did you want him for?"

Pretty as she was, she was still a mother — had to know everything.

"I was hoping he'd take a look at my bike for me," I said.

She laid her hand on the screen-door latch without opening it. "He's just changed his clothes," she said. "Was he expecting you?"

"No. I was just passing by and thought . . ."

She had a smile like David's, one that hung around the corners of her mouth in little creases. "David didn't say anything about anyone who rides a bike. Where do you know him from?"

Despite the smile, I could tell she was sussing me out, especially the holes in my shirt and my jeans. All bike-riders dress like this! I crunched my boots in the gravel, leaned my helmet on one hip and said in my deepest voice, "I'm Vince's brother."

"Oh." She tucked her book under her arm. "Yes, David has mentioned you."

Being merely mentioned still wasn't going to get me in to see him.

"His father's going to be here any minute to take him into town," she said. "I'm afraid he won't have time to look at your bike." It had to be the world's nicest brush-off. "I'll tell him you called if you like."

"Nah, it doesn't matter," I said.

Then David called from one of the inside rooms, "Mum, is this shirt clean?"

She turned away, presuming I'd go, I suppose, and answered him: "Yes."

"You don't know which one I mean," he called.

She stepped away from the door. "If you got it out of your wardrobe, it's clean. And I can't see you getting a shirt from anywhere else."

David stepped into the hall and just about flood-lit it. His shirt, hanging loose over his jeans, was whiter than white. "Look at this. There's a mark on it," he said.

His mother took the cloth between her fingers and pulled it toward her, pretending she needed to strain her eyes to see.

"If you mean that, it's probably grease," she said.

"It can't be grease. I've never worked in this shirt," he told her.

71

He towered over her. She only came up to his second button. His shirt wasn't done up, and his chest showed through, pale and smooth.

"If it didn't come off in the wash, it must be grease," she said. "And if you continue working in your good clothes, they're all going to end up with marks on them." She wasn't angry, she was just ticking him off.

"I never work in my good clothes," he said.

To let him know I was there I moved one boot in the gravel. He looked up, seeing clear over the top of his mum's head.

"Peter?" He squinted through the mesh screen. "Is that you?"

"Yeah."

His mother looked around, annoyed that I was still there. She said to David in a low voice, "I told the boy you were going out. Your father'll be here any minute."

He started doing his buttons up.

"Aren't you going to put on another shirt?" she said.

"No, this one's fine. I only wanted to know if it was clean. Thanks, Mum." He stepped around her, opened the door latch with his elbow, and came outside.

And she came out after him. "Tuck your shirt in," she said, and tried to tuck it in for him.

"Mum!"

She didn't look so young out in the sunlight. There were lines across her forehead, and a few deep ones round her eyes, probably from having embarrassed herself. She smiled to try to make up for it, and he tucked his shirt in like he'd been going to do all along.

His hair was gelled, and he must have just shaved because the usual dark line around his chin wasn't as noticeable.

"I didn't expect you till Friday," he said to me. (That was the day we'd arranged that I'd take the pictures for him.) He told his mum, "Peter's going to take some photos of my car for me."

Her mouth tightened; she was annoyed again. That wasn't the reason I'd given for coming to see him.

"Actually, I came about something else," I said quickly. It hadn't occurred to me that I'd make things awkward for him by turning up on his doorstep. "I was wondering, instead of paying me for the photos, would you mind taking a look at my bike? It needs tuning. At least I hope that's all it needs. I've tried doing it myself but I only make it worse."

David passed his hand through his hair, messing it a bit. "I don't know much about bikes, but for what it's worth," he said, "I'll take a look at it for you."

His mother rattled the door handle. "Not in that shirt!"

"I'll only *look* at it, Mum. Cross my heart." He crossed the whole of his chest with a slow, graceful finger.

There wasn't much she could say to that, and she seemed to realize it. She pulled her book from under her arm and took a bite out of her apple. "Just don't forget, your father'll be here soon."

"I won't." He stepped down on to the path and his mum went back inside. "Where's your bike?" he asked me. He seemed happy enough to see me.

"In your driveway," I said.

He waved me forward. "Lead the way."

— 16 —

I started my bike in the driveway and stood next to it, working the throttle to keep it firing. Out in the sunlight, David's shirt was snow-blinding. Or it could have been the sight of my bike rattling on its side-stand like a three-legged washing machine that made him squint so hard.

"Who's your mechanic?" he asked.

"Me!" I said.

"Got any other career options in mind?"

"I'd like to make movies," I said.

"Good idea, make movies." He stepped away. "Put that thing out of its misery. I'll get some tools."

"I've got some here," I said.

They were in the pouch at the back of the bike seat.

"Thanks. I prefer to use my own," he said.

When he brought them from the garage I could see why. They were chrome-plated, and he carried them wrapped in a rag almost as clean as his shirt.

He bobbed down beside the bike, fitted a socket head over the sparkplug, and gave it a wrench to unseat it. I bobbed down next to him.

"Mind if I watch?"

"No."

I put my helmet on the ground and leaned on it.

Most of his height must have been in his legs, because

down on our haunches like that, our faces were on about the same level. He wound out the sparkplug and frowned at it.

"Oh, I had it out the other day!" I remembered to tell him. "See?" I showed him the smear on my jeans.

"Then it is oiling up?"

"Is it ever!"

"Good. For a minute there I thought you had big problems."

"Nothing a new bike wouldn't fix?" I said, and he grinned.

I liked this bloke; he appreciated my sense of humor!

He cleaned the plug head and sandpapered the contact points, and got grease on three of his fingertips doing it.

"Don't get grease on your clothes," I said to him, and he said, mock-serious, "No, Mum."

I liked his sense of humor too.

Funny, but the last time I was with him my head wouldn't stop telling me: He's queer! He's a poof! He does it with blokes! Now, a mere three days later, I had to keep reminding myself: Don't forget he's gay! Play it cool with him! And go easy on pointing out oil smears on your thighs!

He reset the gap. When he was ready to wind the plug back in, I handed him the socket, and our fingers touched. I felt a bit like the checkout chick in The Markets — I'd done it intentionally. What was it like to touch a bloke who was gay?

David didn't read anything into it, he just said, "Thanks." When he had the sparkplug back in the block, he said, "Want to start it up again?" and stood back while I pumped the kick-start.

The bike was filthy, with mud caked along the chassis and weeds caught in the guards. David's hands, by comparison, were scrubbed clean. And if I'd thought he handled a knife and fork with delicacy, his touch on a screwdriver was mesmerizing. He held the handle in one hand, just taking the weight of it, and actually turned the screwdriver with his other hand, rolling the shaft between his fingertips.

He turned the idle screw, eased the revs up to the thousand mark, and left them there. Then he swapped the screwdriver over to the mixture screw and pivoted it back and forth, getting the feel of it. I love watching people do things really well like that. It hypnotizes me, I could watch for hours.

The bike didn't shudder so much now, but it roared louder. Slowly, David started cutting back the fuel intake, and although the engine was blatting away only thirty centimeters in front of his face, he leaned closer to listen to the fall of the engine note. With his head forward, his hair hung loose in the breeze. Out in the sunlight, the one blond hair looked white. Maybe it wasn't dyed, maybe he was going gray. At twenty?

He kept his lips together and breathed through his nose, concentrating hard, cutting the mixture back slowly, then feeding it again, then cutting it back, paying my grotty old bike more attention than it deserved. I didn't ask questions; I just listened too.

A car pulled up to the curb at the end of the drive and a bloke got out.

"That's Dad," David said.

He was nowhere near as tall as David, and was much bigger built, stockier. Half his face was covered by a black beard with gray streaks in it, and generally he looked pretty fearsome. He parted his suit coat as he walked toward us, and stopped with his hands on his hips.

"I thought you wanted to go to town," he said.

Except for the beard, you'd have thought he was a policeman.

"I do," David said. "This'll only take a minute." He introduced us. "Dad, this is Peter Dawson, Vince's brother. Peter, this is my dad."

Because David had made it kind of formal, I felt obliged to stand up. Mr. Rutherford offered me his hand and we shook. He had a riveting grip, and the eyes above the beard were pretty riveting too. My grotty bike gear was being sized up again, and the rips and tears were rating badly.

"Peter's a photographer," David explained. "He's going to take some pictures of my car for me."

Mr. Rutherford gave me my hand back. "So you're Vince's brother? You two don't look much alike."

"No. Vince takes after Mum. I take after Dad." That's not something I usually admit to, but this guy with his suit, and his beard with gray stripes like tusks, was pretty intimidating. I had to say socially acceptable things, make *serious* small-talk.

"Are you younger or older than Vince?" he asked.

Now I was getting the third degree!

"Younger," I said. I didn't tell him how young. I wished he'd go away, he was making me feel like slime. And I wanted to watch what David was doing! I wanted to be able to tune my bike myself one day.

"What model is this?" he asked, nodding at the bike. I told him and he said, "They don't last long nowadays."

David kept turning the screwdriver, cutting the mixture further and further back until the carbi was drawing almost pure air and the engine was wheezing.

"You'll lose it," his dad said. "And if you do, you'll have to feed it to get it going again, and I don't have that sort of time. I've got a meeting with the Unions at twelve."

So shoot through!

Two lousy minutes of David's time, that's all I wanted! But I couldn't bob down and watch, I couldn't even talk to him now. His old man had thrown a *blind* around him.

Don't you have an airplane somewhere you can go off and fiddle with, mate?

I wasn't even allowed to answer questions. David fed fuel back into the carbi and asked, "That sound OK to you?"

His father answered: "Sounds fine."

He'd taken one look at my clothes and classed me as a hoon. I'm not stupid, I know what people are thinking. He thought I was hanging round his precious son, after a quick thrill. *As if we could get up to much in the bloody driveway!*

David played the revs back and forth, making sure they were in the right spot.

"With an old bike like that," his father said, "that's as good as you'll get it." Neither my bike nor I were worthy of his son's attention.

David brought the idle back down, stood up, and rapped the throttle a few times to make sure it wasn't sticking.

"Smoke look all right?" he said.

I got in first this time. "Looks terrific!" I said. It was

a nice hazy blue and it was wafting away over his father's car. "I thought you said you didn't know anything about two-strokes?"

"He's pulled enough lawnmowers apart to be an expert on them by now," his father said.

David smiled sheepishly and sucked at his lower lip.

His dad looked at his watch. "If you want those brake shoes . . ."

That was my cue to get lost. I pulled my helmet on.

"Do you ride on the road?" Mr. Rutherford asked as I turned the bike around.

"I've only got to go as far as Longworth," I said.

"It's still a public street, and that bike's not registered."

That's right, Pop. I'm a delinquent! A law breaker! A hazard to the community! Got ya scared?

David leaned toward his father and said quietly, "It's his bike, Dad. It's got nothing to do with us."

God, it must be wonderful to be taller than your old man!

"Catch ya later," I said, and as I rolled past David, he winked and said, "Take it easy, Ace."

I rolled the bike out of the driveway on to the road, crossed the double center lines, and gunned it. And felt the front lift! It hadn't done that for ages. I threw my weight back, snapped up hard on the handlebars and brought the wheel straight to the balance point. It hung there, on a level with my head, turning slowly.

I hadn't chucked a wheelie for ages, not since the accident. That's how I'd had the accident — three months back, I'd flipped it. But it was like I'd never left off. All my actions were automatic: my wrist feathered the throttle, my boot covered the back brake. I straightened out my legs and watched the road stream beneath

79

me. I even turned the front wheel sideways for effect.

OK, I was showing off, but I wanted to show that I was good at something too. I blipped the throttle to keep my speed low — did it without thinking, really. My arms ached from being out of practice, otherwise I could have held it up forever.

A car passed me, going the other way, and the driver's eyes bulged out like hardboiled eggs. I guess a bike standing one and a half meters in the air, coming straight at you with all its plumbing exposed, is quite a sight.

I felt the road curve away beneath me. Longworth would be coming up soon, and wheelstanding downhill is a whole new stunt. I let the revs fall. The front wheel floated down and kissed the tar. I leaned through the corner and glanced back to see David standing out on the footpath. His white sleeve came up as he waved. I couldn't wave back, it was one of those moments when I needed both hands.

Anyway, his old man was with him — his bodyguard in a business suit.

I must have hit eighty going down Longworth. I was flying. My shirt tail snapped behind me.

17

I flew into the paddock, taking the bump at the gate head on. A couple of kids hooted me and I thumbed them up. The bike was purring! I rode across the flat, slowing down only to check out Gaz's hill-climb.

It was a well-defined track now. It snaked up the slope to finish at Mr. Grimley's back fence, and it was quite a haul. Gaz hadn't picked the easiest spot to cut it. There were no trees to dodge but there were no rest spots either. It went more or less straight up, and dead in the middle was a granite boulder about the height and size of a car. Nothing a decent bike couldn't get over, but if you were set on losing your life up there . . . yeah, you could do it.

Not all the boys had opted to try it, I noticed. A handful were cruising the flat, circling like sharks, just using up petrol and watching the others.

The novelty of the climb had worn off in a couple of days, and now they were using it as a downhill run. Nothing lasts long with these kids. I hoped the business with me and Eddy on Friday had died the same death.

I stopped on the flat to watch Jason power his little RX80 away from the top. He wrung the gizzards out of the motor, making sure every window along Valley View quaked. The track was fresh and soupy, a mixture of dirt and churned-up weeds, and he fishtailed down the first half of it, not necessarily keeping to the run.

When he came to the boulder, he launched himself off the edge with a slight twist that got more and more pronounced as he sailed further out into the air. I could see his shoulders working as he struggled to straighten himself out. He's going to lose it, I thought, he's going to pancake! Fortunately the RX80's pretty light, pretty easy to toss around, and on touchdown some fancy footwork saved him.

Which was just as well. Slacko was right behind him, bearing right down on top of him.

These kids are stupid! If Jason had lost it, they'd both have been mangled.

Gaz sat at the top of the climb on his green Husqvarna, organizing everyone else to come down. *He* didn't have to, he was Gaz, the chief! Of course, he would have been up and down it a dozen times himself already, but he was still making a big deal about directing the traffic and being the one in charge. That's why I had to deliver my message to him and no one else. I had to look like I was willing to face him.

And I was! I knew exactly what I was going to do: say my piece and leave. I hadn't been to the Westfield bush for ages, and with the bike running so well, that's where I felt like riding. It didn't matter to me whether these kids rode the bloody hill or not. They could break their necks for all I cared. Some of them I could happily live without.

If Gaz was going to sit at the top of the climb all day, that's where I'd have to go to do my talking. I didn't mind that either. I knew it'd look good, me turning up there voluntarily. And I'm as good a rider as either Jason or Slacko. If they could run that hill, so could I.

I was about to take off when the sharks tore past me across the flat, homing in for the kill, yelling:

"Here he comes!"

"They got him!"

"Go, Alice!"

I couldn't believe it. There was Eddy Peterson wobbling down the first few meters of the slope, walking his bike rather then riding it, digging his heels in and straining back on the handlebars. He was going so slow his own smoke was overtaking him.

"Ride 'em, cowboy!"

"Go, Alice!"

The boys cheered him on, eager to see real live blood trickling down the slope. The way he was sliding toward the boulder, more under the power of gravity than anything else, they were going to get it.

Eddy's face was white and his pimples were neon. My own palms started sweating on my handgrips just watching him. *Dump it, ya fool!* If he came to the boulder like that, he'd drop right off the edge.

At the crucial moment, as he was about to take a nose-dive into oblivion, he dropped out of sight. He reappeared seconds later on the track below, still wobbling, still digging his heels in.

There'd been a detour. He hadn't been in *real* danger. But his face was streaming and his eyes were raspberry jelly when he reached the bottom of the climb. His bike had cut out somewhere on the lower slope and he came across the flat pushing it with his feet, like a kid on a tricycle.

The boys pulled in around him and pushed their bikes with their feet too, mimicking him.

"Have a nice ride, Alice? Give ya a thrill?"

"What's up, Alice?"

Blubber dripped off his nose on to his petrol tank.

"Check out his pants!"

They sniffed around him like a pack of dogs.

I know he asks for it, being such a drongo, but, geez, he never asked for this.

I eased off my handbrake and let my bike roll forward. "Why don't yus leave him alone?" I said as I came near them.

"Look who's here, Alice. Ya poofy boyfriend's here!"

"Come to give ya a cuddle!"

"Knock it off," I said.

Eddy looked punch-drunk. His eyes were glassy, his head wobbled like it was attached to his body by an elastic band.

"We all know about you!" one of the kids said, a Year 8 midget who'd just started riding with the group.

"Deadshits!" I mumbled.

These were mostly younger kids and they all looked half demented.

Then Eddy saw me. His eyes came into focus, his mouth gaped open, and he yelled in a voice pitched to shatter plateglass, "We all know about you now! Everyone knows about you!" He sprayed blubber everywhere.

Stuff you, mate! And I'd come across to help! *Forget it, turkey, you're on your own!* I powered away.

I rode up over the old pit head and found myself streaking through the undergrowth tunnels at top speed, which is not a good idea. There's not enough room to pass in the tunnels, and we've never made any rules about them being one-way. We've made no rules about anything in the paddock. Mum doesn't know the real dangers here. She thinks it's just the bikes.

I came out into the open near the highway, and in front of me the long line of back fences curved around the top of the ridge. I picked my way along them, past piles of garden rubbish people had tossed over their fences, out of sight. I passed our back fence. Vince'd be inside, the biggest worry of his life being the size and location of his next pimple. I could picture Mr. Grimley on the other side of *his* fence, yelling into the phone, trying to make himself heard above the blat of bikes congregating on his property line.

It was a stinking day. The air above the paddock was brown. You could see right across Westfield from up here, and there wasn't a cloud in the sky. And none of the civilized trees hanging over the fences was giving any relief. There was no shade.

Gaz and Rats and half a dozen others watched me roll toward them. Jason was back up at the top again too. No one seemed to be saying much. Even Gaz was at a loss for something to do, waiting for me to get there. He fiddled with his gloves, slapping them against his thigh.

I didn't have any choice over where I pulled in among them. It was only a narrow space, and the one vacant position was the leaping-off spot at the top of the hill, so I pulled up there, with the slope literally falling away from under the tread of my front wheel.

I tried to look unfazed, and hoped no one would notice my knuckles turning white as I held on to the handbrake lever. *Never look scared.* Your guts might be running down the insides of your legs, but you must never *look* scared. That's survival.

Below us, Eddy sat with his head between his knees and his bike lying beside him on the ground. Probably he'd never get on it again. The way the boys were grinning told me that, having notched up one success, they were itching for another. They expected me to take one look at the track from the top and chicken out. And, I have to admit, that black dirt slippery-dip, sloppy as mashed banana, pitching down the slope, vanishing into nothing off the edge of the boulder, *was* a pretty gut-draining sight.

Slopes always look meaner from the top, I reminded myself. And when you've never been down them before, too. But if Clinton and Eddy could make it . . . ! I had to be careful not to let *their* judgment of me affect what I knew I could do.

The boys like to think I can't ride, but I can! I'm not a tough guy or a deadhead like them, but I can handle a bike OK, and that bugs them. I've ruined the image, see? They'd run me out if they could. Maybe that's what they were after.

"Come to try our little hill-climb?" Rats smiled, showing the points of all his miniscule teeth.

Most of the boys smirked and exchanged glances, keeping each other on-side. Gaz sat more or less on his own. If I stayed in good with him, I'd be all right.

"Hate to tell yus this, fellers," I said, sort of in his direction, "but the phone's been running hot. We've been getting calls about bikes along the fences . . . about the noise."

"So?" Rats said.

Jason did the same, pushed his face forward and said, "So?"

With so many bikes in a tight space there wasn't much

oxygen to spare, and I had to remind myself to breathe slow and deep. My own bike was chugging nicely: I had my escape hatch if I needed it.

"Someone's called the cops, too," I lied, "and the word is, we're not supposed to ride up here."

"So what are *you* doing up here?"

"Watch out for your mummy! She'll sneak up on ya with her big whip and get ya!"

"Reckon that's who he musta took after, his mum!"

As usual, everyone had to say something.

"Gunna run 'im through the test too, Gaz?" Jason sniggered.

Gaz looked at me from under his stubby red eye-lashes. "Tut-tut, Dawson," he said. "The things we've heard about you. I am truly surprised."

"I'm not!" Rats yelled.

What could they have heard? There was nothing *to* hear!

My hair prickled inside my helmet. A drop of sweat began to slide down the side of my face and I wiped it away fast. No way did I want it mistaken for a tear. They weren't going to reduce me to blubber.

"Have fun with your friend the other day, Petra?"

Petra? That was new, and ominous.

"Got a new boyfriend?"

"Alice's gunna be heartbroken."

"Ya were seen!"

"Always had me doubts about you!" Jason yelled.

Rats went one better. "*I* never did!" My bike shook: the little runt had kicked it. "And I ain't riding with no poof!"

"Don't take it out on me just 'cos yus aren't allowed to ride up here!" I said. "I'm not allowed either!"

"Ya were seen!"

"Out with your boyfriend, shoppin'!"

"D'ya have fun with the carrots?"

I'd been seen with David.

Shit! Had they seen him leaning on my shoulder? *Who* had seen me?

They didn't know David, they didn't know he was gay, I was sure of that. If they did, he'd have been part of their conversation long ago. They were drumming this up out of nothing — just because we'd bought groceries together.

I bad-mouthed them straight back, told them *they* were poofs, made it just words. They were better at this than me, they came up with better filth.

Gaz didn't join in, I noticed. Maybe he was waiting to see how I handled it. I sat rock solid, staring out over the paddock. If he backed me up, I'd be out of trouble. But how did I get him to do it?

You're right! That guy you saw me with was a dead-set poof! Even in The Markets he tried to feel me up. Admit it, entertain them with the details. Join ranks with them.

Throw David to the wolves.

I had a bad taste in my mouth, the taste of bike fumes. The air was thick with them.

He's a friend of my brother's. My brother sent me off with him.

How many people did I have to dump here?

"We'll have t' announce it in school assembly," Jason said. *"Will all the boys in the vicinity of Peter Dawson please watch their backsides . . ."*

They wouldn't do that exactly, but I knew what they would do. Pin notes on the school bulletin board about me. Write my name on every toilet door, and my phone number too. My bag would become the lunchtime football. I'd get jostled on the stairs. Everywhere I went, there'd be a foot sticking out, trying to trip me.

I knew the routine. I'd seen it happen before, to kids who got labeled. I'd seen Tony do it.

"Run 'im out!" Rats yelled.

I noticed that the sharks down on the flat were staring up at us, eyes shaded, mouths open. Everyone had been prepared for this but me.

"Kick 'is head in!" Rats tried for more.

The price you pay for winning the English prize. Is it worth it?

Gaz sat squat on his bike, every part of him protected with leather and buckles and zips. Every part of me was exposed in frayed jeans and a holey shirt.

I knew better than to plead. "Deadheads," I said. "Yus wouldn't know a poof from a lamp post."

"Ain't he tough?"

"Show us how butch ya are!"

"Bet he can't make it."

"Geez, even Alice made it down the hill."

They were enjoying themselves, laughing it up. I couldn't just sit there: I had to fight back, even if I had no hope of winning.

"You're all real big men when you're all friggin' together!" I said.

"Would ya rather get us one at a time?"

"Who do ya fancy best?"

"Me! He likes me!"

They rocked on their bikes, pulled faces, speared each other in the ribs. Rats kept on trying to convince them I should be bashed: "Mince him!" But they didn't go for that, they waited to see what Gaz would do.

89

"What d'ya reckon, Gaz?"

"Mm?" He looked up, sleepy-eyed, like he'd been thinking of something else, something more important.

"What d'ya reckon about Dawson?"

I felt my fate drop into his lap like a football. Gaz played his moment of power to the full. He sucked his bristling moustache and eyed me up and down. He knew what the boys wanted him to say, and for all his posing and being in charge, I reckon he didn't dare *not* say it.

"Hmmm, definitely poofter material, fellers. You're goin' to have to watch yourself round here."

"Run 'im out before yus catch somethin'!" Rats was after blood.

"Stay away from the fences or you're out!" I yelled. I had to say something. Unfortunately, my fabulous imagination goes blank at times like these, and that's all I could think of. My insides were knotted. I slammed the throttle over, the bike leaped forward, and next thing I was falling through space, leaving my guts behind.

My tires hit dirt and I was racing! Downhill, fast, fishtailing all over the place. I went for raw speed to straighten me out, and it did. But I was going *too* fast. All I could see was a moving square of muck and tangled weeds disappearing under my front tire. I had no idea where I was on the hill; when the boulder would appear; whether I was on line for it. I backed off the gas and wobbled all over the place. I had to gun it, or lose it.

I didn't blink. Didn't breathe. There wasn't time. The boulder came out of nowhere. First a tiny flat spot, then . . . flight! The ground wasn't there and the engine was screaming beneath me. I strained every muscle in my body to keep the bike straight-on and the front wheel high.

I rode on instinct. Felt every rubber ridge on the hand-grips, felt every speck of dirt on my teeth. I touched down hard, the suspension bottomed out, but the bike sprang up and kept hurtling forward. It did everything I asked it, thank God!

No, thank David!

I was only just in control and that's all; right on the outside edge of what I could do. An extra few revs, the smallest rock in the wrong place, the tiniest insect hitting my face could have written me off.

I came off the bottom of the slope at a ridiculous pace and suddenly there was Eddy Peterson running toward me like a windmill, his arms and legs gyrating and his mouth yelling, "I saw ya at The Markets! I saw ya!"

Him! I could picture it, too: his eyes peering over a tray of turnips, not believing their luck at what they saw.

I'd happily have run him down, but I knew it'd kill both of us if I hit him. When he realized I was going too fast to pull up, he stopped dead, covered his head with one hand, his balls with the other, and just stood there.

I threw the bike into a slide and nearly broke my ankle doing it. I felt my foot twist inside my boot as I slid past his kneecaps, missing him by a bootlace.

He couldn't see that I'd saved his life, all he knew was that I'd sprayed him with stones. So he ran after me, picking up handfuls of dirt and throwing them at me, screeching, "Poofter! Poofter! Poofter!" till his voice cracked.

I didn't bother going on to the Westfield bush. I just went home.

18

Tony phoned Wednesday to let me know the girls were coming at two. Then he turned up early with them. He bounded up the stairs, yelling. "Where are ya!"

I was in my bedroom looking for a comb so I could do my hair.

"They're in your garage, mate. Come on, move it. This could be your last chance."

"My last chance at what?"

"At getting a girlfriend, dickhead! That business about you being a poof is headlines."

". . . So?"

"*So!* If the chicks get wind of it, you're through. Finished! You might as well be a poof for all the action you're gunna get. Score a girlfriend now, while you still can, and prove 'em wrong."

"I don't have to prove anything, Tony."

"Don't be a jerk, of course you do."

"Rats calls everyone a poof," I said. "It doesn't mean a thing."

"It's not just Rats!"

"I still don't care."

"D'you want every creep at school sniffin' after ya? D'you wanna get locked in the sports closet with Malco? Get a girlfriend, that'll fix everything."

"I don't know any girls."

"Ya know Sophie."

"Hardly!"

"She likes ya . . . Well, put it this way, she likes ya now."

"What's that supposed to mean?"

"Nothin'."

"Tony!"

"I put in a good word for ya, OK? I told her you fancied her."

"Bloody hell! What'd you do that for?"

"To get a bit of action going for ya! You won't do anything for yourself. She likes ya! She likes it when you wear shorts to school. She pervs on your legs! She told me so!"

If I'd been wearing shorts at that moment, I'd have changed out of them.

"You should have kept your mouth shut!"

"It worked! She's all spiffed up. She's wearing a dress."

"What's that got to do with it?"

"Everything! It means she's itchin'! It means all you gotta do is go down there, crack a few funnies, hand her a few lines, give her a quick feel-up, and she's yours."

"Tony, this is your sister you're talking about."

"She's gotta do it with someone, it might as well be you. At least I know where you've been."

I just stared at him. I couldn't believe it.

"You don't have to tell me about it!" he said. "Just make sure you use frangers. If you knock her up, you'll have to marry her. She *is* Italian."

"I'm not screwin' your sister and that's that!"

"Why? What's wrong with her?"

93

"There's nothing wrong with her."

"I know she's fat," he said.

"She is not fat!"

"See, ya do like her!"

"That's not the point."

"What's wrong with ya?"

"There's nothing wrong with me."

"Anyone'd think I was asking you to jump off a cliff!"

That's exactly what he was asking me to do! Feel up his sister, whip out the condoms and lay her, all before Mum got home!

"Quit pushin' me!" I said.

"Of course, if you're not up to it, fine, don't bother! But I can't keep hanging round with ya if everyone thinks you're a poof. They'll think I'm one too."

"Thanks a lot, *friend*."

"I can't! *You* wouldn't! If it was the other way round, I wouldn't expect ya to."

"You don't know what I'd do, Tony."

"I do!"

"You don't!" I glared at him.

He marched to the door. I thought he was going to stamp out. "All right!" he said, and turned around. "All right, you can have Gloria! And if you say you don't want her, I'll punch your bloody face in."

I didn't know what to say. I didn't want her, but in all the years I'd known Tony, that was the most unselfish thing he'd ever done. I know what chicks mean to him.

"But you gotta tell me about it!" he said.

"And what about Sophie?" I asked.

"Forget her. She'll get over it. Though I'm telling you now," he came back to point his finger at me, "you'd have been better off with Soph. She's more your speed."

Maybe he was right. Maybe a girlfriend for a few weeks was the answer. Take her to the movies, let lots of people see us together.

I had about a hundred dollars in the Building Society. Twenty dollars a movie — five dates. That should be enough, and after that I could tell her I was afraid we were getting too serious and we should cool it.

I didn't *have* to screw her. No one'd know whether I did or not. Only Tony, but he wouldn't blab. We were friends.

"Maybe I should take Sophie," I said.

"Take who you like, but quit fart-arsing around. Your hair's fine. Come on! Quit stallin'. It's now or never."

"What were yus doin' up there? We nearly left." Gloria was sitting back against my bike seat with her legs stretched out in front of her, in jeans so tight she had to ease the wrinkles down them with her hands when she stood up.

"Peter was doing his hair," Tony said. Then, as a lead-in on a compliment, he asked, "Doesn't Soph look nice?"

Deep down he still wanted Gloria for himself, and deep down I was happy for him to have her. The jeans left nothing to the imagination, and she was wearing a skimpy pink top with no bra. Her breasts kind of floated around underneath. That sort of thing looks great in magazines or from a distance, but when you've got to talk to a girl dressed like that, it doesn't give you many places to rest your eyes. And you're never sure how your body's going to react, if you know what I mean, and that's a worry.

I told Sophie I liked her dress. It wasn't as big as the tops she usually wore, and the color matched her lips. She said, "Thanks," and looked at her feet. Then we all stood around for a few seconds, listening to the plumbing creak. I'd been to the toilet before I'd come down, and water still gurgled through the pipes across the garage roof.

Before Tony had arrived, I'd been looking forward to this — showing off my darkroom. It might be dull stuff to talk about, but it's interesting to do, or watch. Now all this other stuff had been loaded on to me: girlfriends and condoms. (We've got a house full of them; Mum brings *them* home from the surgery too.) Everything I needed to become "sexually active" was there — the girl, the gear — all I had to do was take the quantum leap. And Tony, as usual, was racing me toward it at breakneck speed.

"Well, you girls came to see the darkroom!" he said, and yanked the door open, sending the walls into convulsions.

Our darkroom is one of those prefabricated aluminum garden sheds. Dad had figured that sticking one of them in the corner of the garage was cheaper than building a room. He'd lined it himself with black plastic and got a couple of his tradesman mates to hook up the plumbing and electricity. It's not Twentieth Century Fox, but it does the job.

"Are you sure it's safe?" Sophie asked.

"Let's hope not," Gloria said. She slunk in over the threshold, and Tony slunk in after her.

I stood back to let Sophie go in first. "After you," I said.

Again she said, "Thanks," keeping her eyes down, and stepped past me, holding her skirt in close to her legs so it wouldn't accidentally brush me. *This was supposed to be the girl who went into orgasm over my naked thighs? I didn't think so!*

Inside, we arranged ourselves in front of the bench: Tony in one corner, Gloria, then me, then Sophie at the other end. Our darkroom was never meant for four people, so we were a bit cramped. We bumped elbows a lot. Mostly Tony bumped Gloria's.

"Want the door closed?" he asked.

"Not yet," I said. "It gets pretty stuffy in here and I have to set up first."

With its plastic lining, the shed's a regular sweatbox. It was warming up already and we'd only just stepped inside. I hoped my deodorant could handle it.

I started my spiel: "This is the developing solution," and poured it into the tray. "And this is the fixative."

"Poo!" Gloria leaned over the mixtures and wrinkled her nose. "What a pong!"

"I never thought they smelled that bad," I said. "Did you, Sophie?"

"No, I never thought they smelled that bad," she said. At least she was agreeing with me. But she wouldn't budge out of her corner, just stood there with her arms folded. Maybe she'd liked me before, but now she'd taken a second look and changed her mind. Girls do that.

I picked up one of the negative strips I had out ready

on the bench, and Gloria pounced on my wrist. She dug her nails in and twisted my arm right back to hold the strip to the light coming in through the doorway.

"What are they pictures *of?*" she asked.

I let myself be manhandled. "Bikes," I said.

"Aw, kinky!" she grinned.

When she let go of my wrist there were two little dents like a snake bite in my skin.

I threaded the negatives into the enlarger and switched it on, and a picture of a bike beamed down on to the board.

It was one of my best shots. The bike was completely airborne, three-quarters-on, front wheel high. It looked like it was just hanging in the air, no effort, light as a feather.

"Who's that?" Gloria shot her hand into the image.

"Garry Gates. Gaz. He was in Year 12 last year," I said.

"D'you know him?"

"Yeah. I ride with him."

"Really?" She poked at the other negatives on the bench. "Who else ya got in there?"

Tony scowled at me. *What was I thinking of, using pictures of other blokes — "older" boys — for my demo?* To make him happy, I said. "You can close the door now."

He leaped at it, pulled it shut, and the walls crackled around us, leaving us in the dark — totally. My dad did a good job of lining the shed. With the light off, you can't see yourself blink in here.

"Turn the light on, Tony," I said.

He just chuckled, "Claustrophobia, anyone?" He was right: with the door closed you could kind of feel the walls shrinking in, making the space tighter. I was aware of Sophie breathing in the corner behind me, and

Gloria swaying on my other side, occasionally brushing against me, making the hairs on my arm prickle.

"Turn the light on, Tony," I repeated.

"Where's the switch?" he asked.

He knows where it is.

"By the door," I said.

He made slapping noises against the wall. "I can't find it!"

"Don't be so childish!" Sophie snapped.

"Soph's scared of the dark," he snickered.

"No I'm not!"

"Don't worry, Pete'll look after ya. Won't ya, Pete?"

"I love the dark," Gloria whispered, close to my ear. "I like to walk around the house at night with all the lights off and *feel* my way." She started marching her fingernails up my arm, taking little stabbing steps.

"Turn the light on!" Sophie did sound scared.

"I'd better turn it on," I said.

Gloria made a little moaning sound as I reached for it myself.

Under the red light, Gloria's hair had turned black and her skimpy pink top was purple. She was wiggling her fingers in one of the trays.

"What happens next?" she asked, as if trying to hurry things along.

"We print the picture," I said. "Would you like to do it, Sophie?"

Maybe she liked me and just didn't know how to show it.

"No. Let Gloria do it," she said. "She's never done it before."

Can't say I didn't try.

My hands shook as I showed Gloria how to position the paper under the enlarger.

99

What ya got the shakes for? Look, Sophie, he's got the jitters, I expected her to say. But she just stood beside me, making soft humming sounds and shaking her hair so that it rustled against her shoulders.

"This is where you switch it on," I said, showing her the switch on the enlarger.

"Where?" She wanted me to put her hand on it, so I did. The automatic timer started ticking.

"It takes five seconds," I said.

She leaned toward me. "What takes five seconds?" she asked, pressing her breast against my arm.

"To print the image on the paper," I said.

The enlarger clicked off, and the red light overhead blinked out as well.

"Tony!" I said.

Gloria pretended to be surprised, and grabbed my arm, fanging me with her fingernails.

"Turn the light on!" Sophie said.

"I didn't turn it off." Tony's feet shuffled back across the concrete floor. "We must have blown a bulb. Anyone ticklish?"

I expected him to move on Gloria under cover of darkness, but instead he started making ghost noises in his corner. Usually he only does things like that when we're on our own. I felt like telling him to knock it off, quit embarrassing himself.

Gloria pressed more of herself against me. "Are *you* ticklish?" she asked, and from the giggle in her voice I knew what was coming next. Her fingernails speared me in the ribs.

"Actually, yeah, I am, very!" I said, which made her go at it harder. I could be tickled to death by anyone with a soft touch. Luckily she was a post-hole borer, and I was able to put up with it.

I knew that if I was seen taking *her* to the movies, my "poofter" label would drop off overnight. Everyone would automatically presume we'd done it. And probably I'd have to. The word was, she expected sex from the blokes she went out with; and the way she was rubbing herself against me, I believed it.

Tony went from ghost noises to heavy breathing. Poor sod, wanking off in his head about Gloria, while she was wrapping both arms around the back of my neck, rising up on her toes, zeroing in to kiss me.

She found my mouth in the dark and locked on. She moved her head, moved her mouth, made noises, did all the work. I could have just stood there if I'd wanted to. But I moved my head as well, to show that I was part of this operation too.

She dragged my hand down from her shoulder, pulled it between us and slipped it under her top to clamp it over her breast — soft and squishy, and heavy, kind of, like a balloon full of water. This was not my first kiss, not by a long shot, but it was my first breast, and for a second there I didn't know what to do with it. I knew I was expected to do something, so I gave it a pump.

She liked that and pressed harder against my face, mashing my lips against my teeth. I knew she was trying to force my mouth open, but with all this other stuff going on, I didn't want to have to deal with my first tongue-kiss too. Anyway, I wasn't sure I liked her enough to have her tongue down my throat.

Her mouth was wide open, making a meal of me,

slopping me up. This was more like being eaten than being kissed. She just wouldn't give up. She tried to pry my lips apart. I knew she'd think I was a baby if I kept my mouth closed. I had to open it.

That set her hands moving. They slithered straight down the front of my shirt, over the front of my pants, and *wham!* she grabbed me. The whole lot of me! I nearly went through the ceiling.

I pushed her back hard against the bench. She must have put her hands back to stop herself and flipped one of the trays. I heard it crash, heard the water slop everywhere.

White light spilled over us. Someone had opened the door.

"Me bloody top!" She waved her hands like she'd been splashed with acid. "Look at me bloody top! Ya bloody retard! If this stuff friggin' stains! And look at me stuffin' jeans!" They were streaked with water, too, down the back. "Come on, Soph, there's nothin' happenin' round here, that's for bloody sure!" And, flashing a look at my crotch, she added, "Bloody fizzer!" She shoved me aside to get to the door.

Sophie went after her, head down and hurrying, like a little plump mouse. *Couldn't she make her own decisions about people? Didn't she have a mind of her own?*

Tony glared. "What'd you shove her off for?"

"She bloody grabbed me!" I said, and put my hand to myself like I was in pain.

"I let ya have my bloody chick . . ."

"She never was yours, Tony! Ya never had a hope with her! She's never been interested in you!"

His eyes sliced me into squares of ravioli. Tony can't handle the truth. "I reckon what the kids are sayin' about you must be right. Ya must be a poofter. A chick like that — and you push her away!"

"Piss off, then," I told him. "If I'm a poofter, piss off. You don't wanna be caught hangin' around here!"

"Couldn't ya even get it up for her?"

I could have killed him, standing there looking at me just like she had. I was so angry I couldn't breathe. I couldn't even tell him to get stuffed.

He left in a hurry, banging his shoulder on the doorframe, and judging from the racket it made, it must have hurt. I didn't care. I locked the door behind him, pulled a stool from under the bench and sat nursing my balls in the dark. I wished Gloria dead, I wished them all dead. My eyes stung; my lips throbbed. They had to be bleeding. They tasted raw.

20

I'm not scared of sex. I want it like crazy. But not like *that*, with someone I don't even like.

Sex has got to be the ultimate in revealing yourself and I don't want to reveal myself to just anyone. I'd like to get to know a girl first before I drop my pants. That doesn't mean I'm scared, it just means I'm choosy.

I would really like a girl I could go out with, take photographs with. We could develop them together, make comments on each others' pictures, suggest ways to make them better, that sort of thing.

We'd get to know each other slowly. We wouldn't

always be holding hands or making out. This girl wouldn't get offended or think there was anything wrong with me just because I wasn't always groping for her tits.

We'd do it eventually, of course, my girl and me. It wouldn't happen because we got drunk or carried away. It'd be special. There'd be candles, and maybe wind-chimes playing.

This girl . . . my girl . . . she'd love me. She'd tell me really softly, with her lips against my shoulder so I'd feel the words as well as hear them. I'd love her too. We'd tell each other everything. There'd be no secrets.

She'd move in with me after a while, or at least stay over with me on weekends until we were old enough to get a place of our own. Mum wouldn't like it, my girl sleeping with me in my bedroom, but Mum wouldn't have a choice. This was my life. Our life. The rest of the world could go hang.

21

Dad dropped in on Thursday night, right at dinnertime. It didn't throw Mum, she just steamed up more veggies to make the casserole stretch further.

He sat where David had sat the Friday night before, opposite me. He was wearing his latest Le Coq T-shirt and the light above the table cast half-moon shadows under his biceps and pectorals.

Dad used to be a professional footballer. Now he owns a sports store and works out, runs and generally keeps himself pumped up. But all his "chasing his body around the block," as Mum puts it, hasn't stopped his hair from falling out. He used to have as much hair as me once. Now all he's got left is a thin, bristling crewcut over his suntanned skull. (That worries me!)

After bragging about how his fantastic coaching got the Bar Beach Under-Fifteen Life Savers into the State Comps, he finally got around to the reason for his sitting there eating our dinner. It seems one of his Leagues Club cronies had phoned him to let him know that my name was spray-canned all over the Westfield Mall bus shelter, advertising that I was a poof and my services were available at two dollars a hit.

"You know, if you need more pocket-money, Ace . . . !" Vince said.

"That's enough from you!" Dad jabbed his knife in Vince's direction.

"He was only joking, Dad," I said.

Vince always cracks funnies when Dad's around, to keep things from getting too serious. And to get up Dad's nose.

"Did you know about this, Peter?" Dad asked me.

"About the bus shelter? Yeah." Actually, it was the first I'd heard of it, but I'd been expecting something like that to happen.

"Do you know who put it there?"

"Probably some of the boys I ride with," I said.

Dad just about whipped out the notebook and pencil. "Which boys? What's their names?"

"You wouldn't know them," I said.

"I might." He thinks he knows everyone.

He demanded names. I gave him names: "Slacko, Rats, Gaz . . ."

"They're not names, they're personality disorders," Vince said.

"I told you!" Dad pointed his knife again.

"I think I've got a right to make comments at my own dinner table," Vince said, looking to Mum for support. And she asked him very nicely to pass the butter please.

Dad and Vince don't get on. We were playing with matches once and accidentally set Grandma's shed on fire, and because Vince was the eldest, he got the blame. Dad gave him an awful hiding; I remember being terrified just watching. Vince would have been ten at the time, but he doesn't forgive things like that.

"Whoever put it there could be charged," Dad said. "Defacing public property's a criminal offense."

"It could have been anyone," I said. "I'm only guessing it was the boys."

That's the truth. I didn't know *what* was being said about me round the neighborhood. I'd been lying low. I hadn't been out on the bike since that day in the paddock, and I hadn't heard from Tony since yesterday. It could have even been him who did it.

Dad inhaled, stretching his T-shirt to the limit. "Yes, well, I'll get Dale down at the Council to have it painted over."

"It'd be better to leave it there," I said. "It'll only get painted up again — bigger next time."

If the boys thought they'd got a reaction, it'd be on every bus shelter from here to Wallsend.

"It's coming off!" Dad said. "I don't want your name up in public like that for everyone to see."

106

"Is it Peter's name or yours you're concerned about?" Vince asked.

I thought that was pretty brave.

"It's *both* our names," Dad said. "Peter doesn't want that sort of filth bandied around about him, and neither do I."

David's name was never mentioned, but it was like he was sitting there, listening; and even though it would have been pointless saying anything, I still felt like a coward.

"Dale'll be discreet," Dad said.

How did you paint a bus shelter *discreetly?* At midnight, in dark clothes? As if the boys weren't going to notice!

"I'd rather you didn't," I said.

"It's no problem, son. I'll take care of it. So . . ." He raised a loaded fork to his mouth. "How'd this thing get started?"

"Yeah, come clean, Ace." Vince said. "What've you been up to?"

I talked fast; laughed about it. "The kids must have decided it was my turn to get picked on!" I said. "They're really democratic like that. No one misses out. Everyone gets a turn. Nice dinner, Mum."

"Thank you, honey."

"But there has to be some reason for it," Dad said. "They wouldn't use that name for nothing."

"No, they do! It's what they call everyone," I said. "If you're a bloke, you get called a poof. If you're a girl, you're a slut. It's standard."

"That's right, Bob," Mum said. "Young people invariably attack each other's sexuality. It's their most vulnerable point."

107

"I wouldn't say Peter's sexuality was a vulnerable point," Dad commented.

I don't often agree with him, but on that one — yeah!

"Peter knows what I meant," Mum said.

Dad didn't think so. He likes to think Mum knows nothing about raising boys. Correction — *men!* He looked away from Mum to me again. "Has anything been going on in the paddock I should know about?"

I had my mouth full and just shook my head.

"I know what goes on, son. I know what young blokes get up to. Now, I'm not saying for a minute that I think you'd be involved. No son of mine *would* be! But there's always one rotten apple. We get them in Life Savers. You've only got to get rid of the one."

"Nothing's been going on," I said finally, just to shut him up.

"You know what I mean?"

"Yeah."

"If we've got a problem down there, I don't want to find out about it from anyone else. Understand? I'd want you to be the one to tell me, so I could take care of it quickly."

"Nothing's been going on," I said again.

"If there'd been a problem of that sort in the paddock," Mum said, "I'm sure Peter would have mentioned it."

"There are some topics you don't talk to women about," Dad said. *There are some topics you don't talk to anyone about!* "And he didn't mention the bus shelter to you, or the fact that he was being called that name."

"Perhaps he didn't think it was a problem," she said.

"Or he might have wanted to handle it on his own, Dad," Vince joined in.

"He doesn't *have* to handle things like that on his

own," Dad said. "If there's been any silliness going on in that paddock, I'll take care of it quick smart."

They were all sitting there discussing my life like it was the latest TV soapie.

"All right," I said, "if you must know, I'm being called a poof because *I* had to tell the boys they couldn't ride near the fences. OK? It wasn't my responsibility, I shouldn't have had to do it. They can't stand anyone telling them anything. And now they've got it in for me. They hate my guts. They're callin' me every rotten name they can think of!"

Mum looked sorry, and so she should be!

"You've been called other names as well as that one?" Dad said.

"Yes."

"Such as?"

"I'd rather not say." I sawed through my lamb chop.

"I want to know!"

"They're not names I wanna say in front of Mum." That went down well. Everyone thought I was a great kid for that.

"Have you been called these names to your face?" Dad said.

"Yes."

"You should have flattened the first bloke who said anything."

"Bob! I won't have you coming here advising the boys to solve their problems with violence!"

"That's one of the reasons he's got this problem," Dad said.

"It isn't a problem!" I told him, but of course no one was listening to me any more. They had their own fight to work on now.

109

". . . Because of your silly bloody airy-fairy nonsense about *working things out* and *talking things over*. That's not the way a man does things. A man acts."

"You mean he hits someone?" Mum's not above landing a low blow herself.

"Lynn, I'm not criticizing the way you've raised the boys," Dad said.

"You criticize the way I raise them every time you come here."

"That's not true. I've always said, you've done a fine job. And I know it hasn't been easy."

"No, you don't know, Bob. You're not here to know."

"If I was made more welcome, I might be!"

"No one has made you unwelcome. You're the one who chooses to turn up only when something's gone wrong, so you can flex your muscles and throw your weight around."

"Well, hallelujah, at last you're admitting it — something's wrong!"

"I am not admitting anything of the sort," she said.

"When the whole neighborhood could be thinking your son is queer?"

"Not everyone believes what they read on bus shelters, Bob."

"You can be sure someone's going to jump to the wrong conclusion."

"As far as I can see, you're the only one jumping to conclusions. In fact, I think you're being downright bad-minded about the whole affair."

"You aren't even concerned about what might be going on in the paddock, are you?"

"Frankly, no!" Mum said. "Our boys are intelligent,

they're well informed. I trust them to have a sensible attitude toward these things."

"And what's a 'sensible' attitude?" Dad asked.

"Generally — to accept that a certain amount of sky-larking is a normal part of adolescent development."

"Good God, Lynn!"

"So long as it doesn't go too far."

"I'm glad you added that."

"And I'd like to think the boys trusted us enough to know that, if they came to us for help, we wouldn't over-react!"

This wasn't *over-reacting?*

"Mum, all we do is ride our bikes!" I said.

"So your theory is," Dad ignored me, "the boys can do whatever they like: have girls in their bedrooms, smoke dope . . ."

"Sounds good so far," Vince mumbled.

". . . do *whatever* with their mates, so long as they come home and tell you about it."

"That's not what I'm saying at all," Mum said.

"That's what it sounds like."

He was going red under his suntan; she was going white under her make-up.

"I just don't want them growing up bigoted and guilt-ridden, and alarmed by every difference they come across in other people."

"Can't I even eat dinner without this?" I said. "It's bad enough having the boys on my back without my own family . . ."

"Cool it, Ace."

"I will not cool it! You haven't got people thinking you've been *doing things!*"

"No one thinks you've been doing anything, honey. Your father is simply concerned," Mum said.

"Why are you sticking up for *him* now?"

She closed her eyes, exasperated.

"Yeah, don't look at me, maybe I'll go away!" I said.

"Don't speak to your mother like that," Dad said.

Now they were ganging up on me.

So much for the supportive family.

"Can I be excused, please?" I stood up.

"I'd rather you finished your dinner," Mum said.

"I'm not hungry."

Dad waved me down. "Do as your mother tells you."

"If you don't want to eat that, Ace, I will."

I sat down and went on with my dinner. It tasted like old sneakers.

— 22 —

Vince suggested the subdivision as a good place for taking the photographs of David's car.

"It'll make a good background," he said. "Uncluttered."

We were in our driveway, loading my camera gear into the trunk of the E. H.

"David may not like it," I said. "The kids'll be all over his new paint job."

"You know most of them, don't you?" David asked me.

"My knowing them won't make any difference. They're creeps. Real pea-brains," I said.

"Three of us against twenty of them?" Vince said. "They haven't got a chance." And he stood around smirking, waiting for me to come up with another excuse for not going. What could I say with David there?

When the car rolled into the subdivision, kids came from everywhere, riding across the vacant blocks.

David back-throttled. "I see what you mean," he said, watching as the mob converged on us.

It wasn't too late, we could still go somewhere else.

"In the middle there," Vince said. "That'd be a good place to set up the camera. Then you'd have those long straights to come down and Peter could get some action shots." That's what David had liked most about my photos of the bikes.

We pulled up where Vince said, and from the back seat I watched David go through the slow ritual of switching off the ignition, pulling on the handbrake and unclipping his seatbelt. All with the same graceful movements he'd used at our dinner table the Friday before.

Better keep your hands in your pockets here, mate.

Fortunately, he'd come underdressed that day in a T-shirt, long baggy shorts and hairy legs. Eddy might have recognized him as the bloke I was doing the shopping with, but Eddy wasn't here. Eddy wasn't ever going to be here again. I'd looked in the newspaper on Saturday and, sure enough, there was his bike for sale, going cheap. Not that I was tempted.

The kids were more interested in the car than anything else. They milled around it, making stupid comments.

113

"Ace machine!"

"What a fang!" (Which it isn't!)

One dummy even told David he should paint a picture of a dragon devouring a naked chick on the hood.

"Yeah," David answered in a gruff voice. He knew what he was dealing with now, and he kept his arms folded and his hands tucked under his armpits.

Naturally, he towered over all the pygmies. Gaz was the only one who could have matched him for height, and Gaz was there, but he kept to the footpath, watching from the sidelines. When he was a little red-haired kid in primary school, Gaz was exactly the same: if he couldn't be the center of attention, he didn't want to play.

David answered all the boys' questions about the car, while keeping an eagle eye on handlebars and broken footpegs passing dangerously close to his new duco. I set up the camera on its tripod in the middle of the road, and when I asked him to take the car back along one of the far streets, he went in a hurry, grateful to get away.

A few kids on BMXs trundled after him as he drove off. I yelled at them to keep out of the picture, and that kept them back. I took several shots with the telephoto lens, panning on the car, keeping it in focus while blurring the background. My hands weren't as steady as I would have liked.

From behind me I heard a few snickers about the bus shelter, nothing blatant. It was possible the labeling hadn't stuck as badly as I'd thought. The boys had no *real* reason to think I was gay, it'd all been drummed up out of nothing, and my death-defying ride down the hill-climb might have saved me. After all, it *was* supposed to be the poofter test, and I'd passed it, and half of them hadn't even tried.

Vince being there kept the kids a bit more respectful, of course. He's not physically big but he gives out heavy vibes when he wants to, posing in his sunnies and blowing cigarette smoke out his nose.

I would have had to come down to the subdivision eventually. I wasn't so stupid as to think I could go back to school without putting in an appearance here first, to show that I wasn't scared, and that nothing *they* said was going to faze me. I just would have felt more comfortable doing it my way, in my helmet and boots, with my bike beneath me.

But I was here now, so I concentrated on taking good pictures, and ignored everything else.

It was a top day for photography: bright sunshine, with just a few clouds to cut the glare. Hot as hell, though. All the tar and bare dirt in the subdivision held the heat, and I could feel it rising through the soles of my sneakers.

The kids drifted over to join Gaz on the footpath. It was the usual crowd: Jason, Slacko, Clinton, Joel. Mostly they talked cars. I noticed that Rats was absent. *How lucky can you get?*

When I'd taken enough distance shots, I signaled to David to bring the car back, and he pulled up on the far side of the road, as far as possible from the boys. I still had the telephoto lens on the camera and took a picture of him getting out of the car. Then wished I hadn't. It embarrassed him to death. As he came up to me, he smiled. "Just the car, hey?"

Don't smile at me here! And for God's sake, don't wink!

I got really serious about the photographs after that, took shots from ground level, that sort of thing. Made a spectacle of myself generally, and got ripped off about it.

"Get a load of the hotshot photographer!"

"Smile! It's *Candid Camera!*"

"Gunna take our picture too, Pete?"

Good idea! I swung the camera on them and, through the lens, watched them climb on each other's shoulders and pull stupid poses.

The shutter opened and there, riding in from infinity on a decrepit old bicycle, was Rats. Someone must have gone off and told him we were here.

I turned back to the car and kept on taking pictures, waiting to hear him join the group behind me.

"Where's Alice?" his cackling voice said.

"Alice ain't here!"

"He doesn't know what he's missin' out on."

Etc., etc.

It wasn't the sort of conversation Vince or David could have made any sense of, but the kids snickered a lot.

"How many pictures have you taken now?" David asked, when I'd worked my way back to where he and Vince were standing.

"Sixteen," I said.

"That's plenty. I only wanted one or two."

"No. To get one really good shot, you have to take the whole roll," I said, and I kept on going.

I had to look after myself here. If I shot through the instant Rats turned up, I'd never get him off my back. I fiddled with the light meter, adjusted aperture settings, ignored the heat and the sun biting into the back of my neck, and took pictures.

Only twenty frames to go!

"Spiffy little photographer, isn't he, fellers?" Rats said, and there were mumbles of agreement. The kids were being cautious.

116

Rats never is. "Make a good hairdresser, too!" he added.

I saw David turn his head to glance in Rats's direction.

"Or an interior decorator!"

David's lips moved as he murmured something to Vince. Vince took out his cigarette pack and lit another smoke. This wasn't hurting him; he wasn't in the firing line.

"They go through boyfriends real fast," Rats yelled, "them interior decorators!" There were more laughs. He was picking up supporters.

David stood with his arms folded, squinting a bit. His hair hung low over his eyes. Possibly he heard this sort of thing all the time from the macho engineering blokes at uni.

I cheated, took a couple of shots of the ground, and wandered back. "That's it," I said.

David nodded. "Might as well go then. Do you need a hand to put your gear away?" The only sign he gave of being uneasy was that he jangled his car keys in his hand.

"You reckon he's got a client waitin'?" Rats said. "Wonder how many he's done so far. We should be gettin' a commission. I bet he's makin' a fortune."

I packed my camera in its case and gave it to David to hold, and Vince asked, "Who's the smart-arse with the suicide complex?"

"Rats, his name is," I said as I folded the tripod.

"Is he the one who started it?" he asked.

"Yeah, sort of."

"Is he a friend of yours?" David said. It was a stupid question, but I guess he needed to say something too. I

wasn't sure how much he knew about my problem —
being labeled. I didn't know if it was the sort of thing
Vince would tell him.

"Rats hasn't got any friends," I said.

"Good," Vince said, "you're in luck then. Go surprise
the little jerk. Knock his teeth down his throat."

"No!"

David agreed with me. "His type aren't worth the
trouble," he said.

"These Valley View turkeys sure stick together!" Rats
said. "D'you reckon they've got a clubhouse and go on
picnics? Hey, anyone for a poofter's picnic, leaving
now?" Then he started whistling a song we all knew
from school, one about homosexual stuff: bums for sale,
etc. David probably didn't know it because he didn't go
to school here. But from the way the boys carried on,
snickering, and even acting things out, the joke was
pretty obvious.

"Leave it too much longer, Ace, and you're going to
have to take on the lot of them," Vince said, "not just
him."

David walked away. He didn't want any part of this.
And neither did I.

"You're just like Dad," I said to Vince. "You think
every problem can be solved by thumpin' someone."

"You wouldn't need to thump him if you hadn't
waited this long."

David opened the trunk of the car and put the camera
case inside.

"So where you gunna hide when you go back to
school?" Vince said to me. "The girls' toilets?"

"Geez, David must be hard up for friends," I said,
"having to knock around with you."

"That kid's a bloody dishrag, Ace. Look at him! You're twice his size. Go mop up the subdivision with him."

The boys must have wondered what we were doing, standing there, whispering at each other.

"He fights dirty," I said.

"Fight dirtier! He's got your number and he's gunna hound you to death. You won't shut him up any other way."

"If he bothers you, *you* thump him," I said.

He eyed me off through his tinted lenses, then handed me his smokes pack. "OK. Here, hold these."

"No!"

"Get it over with, then, while I'm here to back you up. Don't be a wimp all your life." He didn't take off his sunnies; he never intended fighting Rats for me, he was just trying to shame me into it.

I glanced at David. Did he think I was scared too?

I'm not usually a doer, so when I act, people often get a shock. Rats sure did.

23

I crossed to the curb, where Rats stood, leaning back on his bicycle, curling his lip and showing his teeth. The boys behind him were goggle-eyed. They knew what was going to happen. Rats was the only one who didn't. He even poked out his chin to ask, "What d'ya want, poof?"

I didn't want to talk, and I knew that whoever got in the first punch had the advantage. So I closed my fist and hit him in the face. His head snapped back, his bike fell over, and his fists came up, flashing out of nowhere.

He got me in the guts. I collapsed forward. If I hadn't had him to hold on to, I'd have ended up on the ground. We stayed more or less in a clinch like that, throwing punches at each other's backs and breathing down each other's necks.

It wasn't much of a fight. We thumped each other, shuffled our feet, and generally made idiots of ourselves. Voices cheered me on: "Go 'im, Pete!" which meant I had to be doing OK. Kids don't back losers. And I know they'd been waiting a long time to see someone give Rats a hiding. I'd never thought it was going to be me.

I kept on banging into him. Vince had been right about him being a runt. Fighting Rats was like doing battle with a box of matches. His chest was narrow and his arms were sticks. The strongest part of him was his stink — like old laundry.

But his knuckles were doorknobs. He landed more punches than I did, and he had a better idea of what he was doing. He systematically pounded every one of my ribs. But of the two of us, I was the heavier fighter. When I did manage to land a punch, it made an impression. It jarred right through him.

Eventually he stumbled backward into his bike frame and fell over and pulled me down with him. We had a rest on the ground then, just scrabbling around, not hurting each other much. Mostly we skinned our elbows on the concrete.

Then the little prick tried to knee me. If my leg hadn't

been in the way, I'd have been in trouble. He'd meant it! And that reminded me that I still had a lot to lose here. I kept on going, letting him have it, both fists, punch after punch, hoping to hell it wouldn't last too long and that I'd know when it was over.

There were noises everywhere, and dust, and people grunting — me and Rats, I suppose. Then suddenly these big colored stars burst right in front of my eyes, and long fiery comets streaked from one side of my head to the other. Geez, it was spectacular!

So was the pain. I thought my head had exploded.

Two hands grabbed me and hauled me into the air, then dumped me on the ground a meter away from where Rats lay tangled in his bike frame. An arm reached down out of nowhere and wrenched a bicycle pump from Rats's grasp. The shiny black hairs showed me whose arm it was. The face that went with it I would never have recognized. David glared down at Rats with twenty thousand volts of electricity running through his eyes. He looked like he was deciding which bit of him to rip off next.

He swung the bike pump back over his shoulder, and Rats's stringy arms flew up to shield his head. So did mine. David sent the pump spinning through the air and the boys grouped in front of us ducked as it sailed over their heads.

Vince hauled me to my feet, and had the sense to hang on to me, otherwise I'd have fallen straight over again. My legs were like licorice.

"Good one, Pete!"

"Seven outa ten!"

"Comin' back for a rematch?"

Even Gaz, holding court from the cushioned seat of

his green Husqvarna, gave me the nod. I was a hero. The fight had amused him.

It'd made me feel like a fool.

Vince walked me to the car and pushed me along the front seat, and got in beside me. David got in the other side. I was sandwiched between them. They clicked their seatbelts in. Even though I could barely see what I was doing, I felt around for mine.

"There isn't one in the middle," David said.

"Living dangerously now, Ace!"

The engine rumbled as the car pulled away, excruciatingly slow. Rats had crawled out of his bike frame and was swaying on his feet.

"You better go faster," I said. "He might throw something."

David's eyes watched the mirrors all the way to the bottom of Longworth. He didn't speed up. He knew the boys better than me: knew they only chased you if you ran.

"So where'd you learn to fight?" Vince asked. "In a pillow factory? Am I going to have to give you lessons in that too?"

"Leave him alone," David said.

"Sir Galahad to the rescue again!"

"He might be hurt," he said, leaning forward to look into my face. I put my hand up to my head, mainly to hide.

"He's all right," Vince said. "A biff on the skull'll do him good." He offered me a cigarette. That was the last thing I wanted. My head already felt like a goldfish bowl.

David parked the car in our driveway.

122

"Come inside and lie down," Vince said to me, "and I'll phone Mum."

"Don't. I'm all right." I got out. "You don't need to phone her. Can we get the stuff out of the trunk?" I didn't want them standing round discussing me. "I'll develop the negatives," I said.

"I'm still phoning her!" Vince said.

"Do what you like. Dob me in," I said.

He went into the house. I got the camera case out of the car. David took the tripod and walked down to the garage with me.

It was nice being in the darkroom, in a closed-in space. It's my hideaway. I started to unpack the camera, but David wanted to look at my head first. Standing in the doorway, he pushed my hair back.

"You're going to have quite a lump there."

"My hair'll hide it," I said.

"Not from your mother, it won't." He touched the spot with his fingertips. "Does that hurt?"

"No. I've got a cast-iron skull. Nothing hurts me."

"Do you feel sick?"

"No."

"Dizzy?"

"Honest, I'm all right!" I shook my head to prove it, and the world swam. I made a grab for the door-frame. David caught me by the arms and his hands felt like vice-grips.

"I'm taking you to the hospital," he said. "You could have a concussion."

"No! Please! I don't wanna go anywhere. I just wanna stay here."

He didn't force me. He walked me back to the bench

and sat me on the stool and said, "I'd better tell Vince."

"Don't tell him anything. I don't want . . . I don't know." I didn't know what I wanted.

I think I'd have been happier if he'd told me to go to hell. It was my fault he'd had to hear all the poofter stuff in the subdivision. We should never have gone there. I should have told Vince straight out that we were going somewhere else. But no, I was too much of a wimp.

Now he was holding me up so I wouldn't fall off the stool. He pulled a wad of tissues from the box on the bench, wet them under the tap, and held them against my forehead, really gently. I was as hot as fire and the tissues were icy.

"You're sure you don't feel sick?" he asked.

I'd made myself look idiotic enough for one day; I was too afraid to talk in case I cried. When he took the tissues away to wet them again, my head fell forward and touched his chest. He didn't push me away. He let me lean there.

"Are you *sure* you're all right?"

He stroked my hair, touching the back of my neck with his fingers now and then. It was the nicest thing anyone had ever done for me. And the softest. He cared — that I might be hurt, that I might fall off the stool.

He put his arm around my shoulders. I put my arms around him and hugged him, pressed my face against his chest and listened to his heartbeat through his shirt.

It was like coming home, like finding the place you've always wanted to be, and I could have stayed there forever holding on to him.

Except I heard Mrs. Minslow gasp, "Oh, my God!" and felt David tighten. Slowly he pushed me away. She

124

stood in the doorway, X-raying us with her eyes. Vince must have told her we were there.

David said calmly, "Now you're here, Mrs. Minslow, I'll leave him with you." He pressed one of my hands on the edge of the bench, giving me something to hold on to.

She stumbled back to let him out the door, watched him go, then shuffled back in.

"What's he done to you?" Her hands raced at me. "I warned your mother about him."

Things flew off the bench — trays, tongs, plastic bottles. And someone — I think it was me — was yelling the same thing over and over: "You fuckin' old bitch! You fuckin' old bitch!"

She disappeared, and I knew where to. She was going to tell the world everything she'd seen. And everyone would believe her.

David's car was gone, the drive was empty, and I didn't want to be there any more either.

My bike made so much racket under the garage ceiling that I was sure it was going to bring the whole house crashing down on top of me.

24

I roared down Valley View. The houses were a blur. The wind whipped my hair into my eyes, making them sting. *No helmet, see.*

At the intersection, I crossed the highway against the lights. Horns blared. I roared up the embankment on the other side and down into the Westfield bush.

It closed over me. I found a trail and followed it through brown scrub. Where it went, I went, past dead cars on their lids, past split garbage bags, down gullies, up hills. I didn't watch my gas gauge or my speedo. I just rode, getting faster all the time.

I won't say I went there to wipe myself out purposely, but on my millionth gully, not a particularly steep one, the front wheel slid from under me, the bike went over, and I went down. No earthquake, no crash: just me and the bike, rattling down the slope, skating over stones. No great pain either, just a sick feeling of being out of control, and my shirt tearing up my back. *Mum's gunna kill me,* I thought. Stupid, isn't it, the things you think of?

Halfway down we slid to a halt under this huge leaning gum tree, and I thought: a place to rest, finally! The bush was quiet, the bike was dead, the only thing to annoy me was bits of gravel trickling into my collar. I could close my eyes and go to sleep.

I smelled the burning before I felt it. There was a split second's difference, and I sat up screaming. The bike was on my leg and the exhaust was burning its way through my jeans. I saw pain in fifteen different colors. Kicked the bike seat, kicked the petrol tank. Started moving again, slithering down the slope with the bike. Eventually it came off me, skinning my ankle as it went. *No boots either.*

I wasn't in the shade any more and my leg felt like someone was holding a blowtorch against it. I wrapped my arms around it and hugged it without actually touching it, rocked back and forth, listening to myself taking huge breaths.

Under the circumstances, anyone would have cried. I didn't bawl, just soaked the knees of my jeans. Why not? I was scratched, burnt, my bike was probably a write-off, and I was probably gay. A girl had kissed me and I'd pushed her away, but a bloke had stroked my hair, and I'd melted all over him. I could have ridden round for a week and never got away from that one.

The boys had seen it. Vince had seen it. I was the only dumb bunny who'd taken fifteen years to notice.

So what did I do now?

Leave school. Leave home. I couldn't stay. Mum'd have a field day trying out her fancy counseling on me. Vince'd think it was hilarious. And when my father tracked me down, he'd murder me for being a "failed" man.

You did this to me, you bastards! I don't know who I was throwing stones at. Anyone. David. He'd seen it in me from the start, that's why he hadn't pushed me away.

He knew I was like him.

25

Peak hour traffic was six lanes thick along the highway when I finally got out of the bush. The patrol cars were out in force with their big white eyes, and I had to walk the bike home, two kilometers along the verge.

There was nowhere to go but home.

Dad's car was parked out in front. Mum's car wasn't in the garage when I wheeled the bike in, but she was, at the bottom of the stairs, wearing a crushed uniform and a face like poured concrete.

"Leave that there," she said, meaning the bike, expecting me to drop it on the floor.

She does this when we hurt ourselves, goes into super-efficient nursing mode. I must have looked a mess, limping in with my shirt in pieces.

Dad stomped down the stairs in his bare legs. He'd come straight from Life Savers and was wearing only a Speedo and a sweatshirt. He took the bike from me.

"And he's never to get on it again," Mum said, pushing me up the stairs ahead of her. "Get rid of it." It was Dad who had bought the bike for me. In the bathroom she pushed me down on to the edge of the bath and checked the lump on my head. So she knew about the fight.

"Have you been sick?" she asked.

128

"I'm fine," I said, shocked that my voice sounded normal. I didn't *feel* normal. I felt I'd come home a stranger.

"I'm not asking you how you are!" she snapped. "Have you been vomiting?"

"No."

She pushed my head back and peeled my eyelids open. Dirt fell out of my hair, spattering into the bath behind me. Staring into my eyes seemed to convince her that I wasn't dead, and after that she settled down a bit.

"Where else have you hurt yourself?" she asked.

I avoided looking at her. "I burned my leg," I said.

I started to roll up my jeans.

"Leave it," she said. "I'll do that." She cut away my jeans with a pair of scissors, and didn't bat an eyelid at the sight of the burn. It made my stomach heave. It was raw meat with pukey white wrinkles. She ran water in the sink and fussed around, getting out creams and stuff.

Vince couldn't have been home, otherwise he'd have been there: *Only one leg, Ace? Not really trying!*

Dad appeared, plugging up the doorway with his bulk. His bright red Speedo peeked from under his sweatshirt and when he raised his hand to grasp the back of his neck I thought: *He knows, and he's going to kill me.*

"All right son, what happened?"

Good God, I was still his son?

"Not now, Bob," Mum said.

"I pranged the bike," I told him.

"I said, not now!"

Dad stepped closer. The smallest room in the house, and he had me trapped in it. "Mrs. Minslow told us what happened." *I knew she would.* "She said he had his arms around you."

Mum was kneeling on the tiles in front of me. "This is going to hurt," she said, and it did. The cottonwool she used to clean around the burn could have doubled as sandpaper.

"I want to know what he did," Dad said.

They were blaming David, not me. The coward in me almost cried with relief.

"He didn't do anything," I said, feeble as a plucked chicken.

"You knew he was a bloody poof?"

I nodded.

"Why'd you let him touch you?"

"He was helping me," I said. "I couldn't stand up. I'd have fallen over."

"He was helping his bloody self. Mrs. Minslow saw him. She said he had his hands all over you."

"Don't bully him, Bob," Mum said.

"Why'd you take off on your bike like you did, without your helmet?"

"I must have forgot," I mumbled.

"It's not like you to forget. Why'd you swear at Mrs. Minslow?"

"I didn't swear at her." I couldn't think fast enough to do anything but deny whatever he threw at me.

"She said you did."

"Why do we have to have her in the house?" I said. "I hate her. She's a rotten old busybody."

"Thank God she was here," Dad said. "Lord only knows what that pervert would have done to you."

"Bob! Peter told you, nothing happened!" Mum said. "Don't you believe him?"

"The way you've raised these boys, they wouldn't know if they'd been molested or not. You've taught them nothing."

She's taught us everything: what to do in case of stranger danger! ringworm! shark attack!

"Can't you see he's hurt? He doesn't need you bellowing at him!" She was the one bellowing now.

"A few scratches? You're carrying on about a few scratches when that mongrel could have given him AIDS! You let him into this house! You put your own son at risk!"

Vince's voice sounded ridiculous as he came into the room, it was so calm. "I see you found him."

Dad spun around. "And where have you been?"

"Looking for him," Vince said. "How is he?"

"He'll be fine when your father leaves," Mum said.

"I'll be leaving soon," Dad said. "Where is he?"

"Who?" Vince asked.

"Your sicko mate."

"If you mean David, he's at home."

"Good. You know he was caught trying to molest your brother?"

Vince knew everything. "Yes, I heard the highly colorful Minslow version," he said.

"He had his arms around him. Cuddling him," Dad said. "That doesn't need too much coloring in."

"David wouldn't molest Peter," Vince said. "He wouldn't molest anyone."

"How do you know?"

"I know him. He wouldn't do it. It's not his style."

"And what is his style?"

"If he's interested, he asks," Vince said.

"How do you know? Has he ever asked you?"

"That's my business," Vince said.

"Ha! D'you hear that, Lynn?" Dad laughed. "He's tried it on with Vince as well."

"He didn't *try it on*," Vince said. "He didn't know if I was gay or not when he first met me, so he asked. I told him it wasn't my thing, and that was that. He's never asked again."

"You mean he put the hard word on you months ago and you're still knocking round with him?"

"Yeah, why shouldn't I? He's a nice bloke, I like him. He's got a right to ask. Everyone's got a right to ask. You do, don't you?"

"Not blokes!" Dad said.

"That's your affair," Vince said. "David's choice of partners is up to him."

"Not when he tries it on with Peter."

"He didn't try anything, Dad," I said.

"He would have if he'd had the bloody chance. But he won't get it again."

"Bob, where are you going?" Mum stood up.

"If you go down there and accuse David Rutherford of sexual assault," Vince said, "his parents will sue you."

"I'm not gunna bother accusing him," Dad said. "I'm gunna wring his bloody neck."

"And what if one of your own sons was gay?" Mum said. "Would you wring his neck too?"

Mum, don't tell him!

"You'd love to throw that one in my face, wouldn't you, Lynn?"

"I'm asking you, Bob, what would you do?"

"Get him away from you for a start," Dad said. "And help him get over it. Tell him what's what! Tell him

132

exactly what's expected of him. Get him into sports. Healthy exercise. All the things you haven't done for these boys."

"What about accepting him as he was?" Mum said. "Couldn't you love him simply because he was your son?"

"No, a man shouldn't have to accept that, being made a laughing stock by his own children. A man shouldn't have to accept that. And that sicko's father down there should have fixed *him* long ago, and not left it for someone else to do."

"If you hurt that boy, neither of your sons will ever speak to you again," Mum said.

"That'd be no great loss with him," Dad said. He waved a paw at Vince. "You can have him. You've ruined him. At least this one's still got some feeling for his father." He reached for my shoulder and I nearly fell in the bath. I didn't mean to pull away. It's just that he's so big, and whatever he was thinking of doing to David, he'd do a thousand times worse to me, because I was his son and I'd let him down.

"I think I'm gunna throw up!" I said.

Everyone scattered, except Mum. She held on to me while I heaved into the bath.

—— 26 ——

On Saturday Mum baked cakes and cookies, all the stuff we've missed out on with her being a working mum.

I stayed in bed mostly, and acted sick. She'd come and sit on my bed and act concerned about my head.

"How are you feeling now, honey?" she'd ask, and I'd say, "OK."

Possibly she'd guessed what was worrying me and wanted me to talk about it. Much as I loved her, I couldn't. Not my mother, not about this.

We talked about Dad. "You know your father loves you," she said.

"I don't think so."

"He does, honey. That's why he was so unreasonable last night. He thought you'd been . . ." She cornered herself there, but didn't try to get out of it. "You know what he thought."

"He was only worried about himself," I said, "and what his friends would say."

"I hope you don't believe that."

"Well, it was part of it," I said. "A big part."

"I know your father can be overbearing at times, but he's still your father. Don't turn your back on him. It's not your place to make judgments about him. He'd never turn his back on you. Look at him and Vince — they don't always see eye to eye, but your father's never withdrawn his support from Vince."

Dad pays Vince's way through law school. And if that was supposed to convince me I could tell my father I was gay and live through the experience, it didn't.

I know Mum was trying to help, but after that I pretended to be asleep whenever I heard her coming. It was easier on both of us.

27

On Monday I caught a bus into town. I took my Building Society passbook with me, and toyed with the idea of never coming back. But just being on the bus was good enough. It gave me a direction, a place to go.

Town was packed: perfect. It meant I was able to walk around, just one of the crowd. It also meant I could check *them* out without being noticed.

Tony told me once that poofters wear blue socks. I don't know who's the bigger dickhead, him for coming up with such a lamebrain idea, or me for actually believing it. Half the blokes in the world wear blue socks!

Maybe there was no one hundred percent certain way of telling if someone was gay.

Then I saw this young bloke come out of a record shop, and he was as camp as they come. You'd have picked it three blocks away, just from the way he walked — kind of wiggling his bum. He was only about my age, too. Did I walk like that and not know it? If I did, all the people behind me in the street would have seen, and they'd know about me, and if they saw this bloke up ahead of me, tripping along, naturally they'd think I was following him, hoping for a pick-up!

I stopped dead in the middle of the pedestrian traffic, did an about-face, and walked back the way I'd come.

No, I ran. I ran the length of the block, then down an arcade, past rows of plateglass windows, watching myself ripple from one to the next. Tony says you can tell poofters by the way they run.

How do they run? Like me?

I kept my arms in close and tried to run in a macho way. Probably I was only exaggerating whatever it was I was trying to hide. People were staring.

At the end of the arcade I ducked into the men's toilets and locked myself in a cubicle. I sat on the bowl, panting, my heart pounding inside my chest like two fists on glass. The graffiti on the door in front of me pressed itself against my eyes: JACKO'S GAY. WHACKA SUX ANYONE.

How did they know Jacko was gay?

There was nothing about being gay in our dictionary at home, or in the encyclopedia. I know, because I'd looked. And there was no one I could talk to.

I'd have loved to talk to David. Everything I needed to know, he knew. But how do you ask about these things? You don't! You can't! If it hadn't been summer vacation, I might have gone to see the school counselor. But a stranger would have been better. I was sure I could talk to a stranger, someone who didn't know me.

OK. I stood up, let myself out of the cubicle and

walked around town again, head down, bum tight, looking for a telephone booth. The one I found had no telephone book, and I had to ask the operator for the number of one of those distressed youth phone-in places. I didn't know what they were called.

"We have several listings," she said.

Tizz-brain, I can't phone several. Give me one!

"There's Youth and Community Services Hot-Line. Life Line Telephone Counseling . . ." I didn't have a pen so I memorized one of the numbers as she rattled them off, and hung up on her.

I dialed again, and listened as my coins fell through the slot. A bloke answered. If it'd been a woman, I'd have hung up. I couldn't have talked to a female about this; it would have been too much like talking to Mum.

"Life Line Telephone Counseling," he said. "Can I help you?"

I draped myself over the phone, so I was speaking right into the mouthpiece, and said, "Yeah, I hope you can. I'm having a bit of a problem."

"Uh-ha?" He sounded old, older than Dad.

"With girls," I said. "Um . . . I don't seem to be doing real good with girls. They don't seem to be doing much for me, if you know what I mean."

"Can I ask you how old you are?" he said.

"I'm fifteen."

Pause.

He wasn't real talkative.

"You sound worried about it," he said.

"I am a bit." *Why else would I be phoning!* "It's not that I don't like girls," I said. "I do. I like 'em lots. On the TV and in *Playboy*, I really go for 'em. But real girls . . .

they're different, they don't seem to turn me on that much. Like the other day, this chick offered to have sex with me and I knocked her back. I didn't want it."

"Uh-ha."

Can't you say anything but "uh-ha"? Have I got a recording here?

"Well, that's not what blokes are supposed to do," I said. "Knock girls back. Is it?" No answer. "And I'm kind of worried about it."

He started talking at last. "You seem to think there's a standard response boys are supposed to have toward girls," he said.

"Yeah."

"And you don't see yourself as matching up to that standard."

"That'd be right," I said. "So . . . what d'you think it means?"

"I don't know if it means anything," he said. He talked slow and calm, as if he had all day. I didn't. Phone booths are made of glass, and some people can read lips. I cupped my hand around my mouth, even though he was doing the talking. "There's no set way of reacting to other human beings," he said. "We're all different, we all respond to people differently."

"You reckon I'm normal then?" I said.

He laughed. "In this job you learn quite early that there's no such thing as normal."

Thanks a lot, feller! I changed the phone to the other ear. "Um . . . there's this other girl, too," I said.

"Oh?"

That made a change from "uh-ha."

"I really like her," I said, "She's nice. I like her a lot, but not in *that* way! I wouldn't wanna screw her."

"And you think you should want to?"

"Geez, any of my mates would. They'd screw any-thing they could get. Anything gets 'em going. They've got it up all the time."

"That's what they tell you."

"I know they bullshit a bit, but . . . well, even if they're not *doin'* it, it's still the way they talk. It's what they'd *like* to do, and that's normal for blokes. And I'm not like that."

"Back to the old question of *normal*," he said.

"Yeah."

Silence. I let it drag. I wanted *him* to talk!

"Let me ask you a question," he said.

Here it comes.

"Would you say you're *under* normal or *above* nor-mal?"

I laughed, and so did he.

"Under, I guess," I said. "I mean, the way my mates are is the way everyone expects blokes to be."

"Your expectations of yourself," he said slowly, "are more important than other people's expectations of fel-lows in general." We were getting serious now. "What's most important is what *individuals* want from their re-lationships with others. And there's a lot more to rela-tionships than sex."

I hadn't phoned up about relationships!

"I know all that," I said. "It's just this thing with girls. It's worrying me. When they don't do anything for you, you naturally think that maybe something's wrong. Maybe you're frigid! Or maybe you're that other way," I hugged the phone tighter, "you know . . . for blokes."

"You sound as if you've thought about it," he said.

"Well, when something like this happens, you think about it, for sure!"

"Perhaps you've had an experience with another lad."

"No way! I've never done anything like that!"

His voice stayed calm. "Or perhaps there's been an instance where you've been sexually aroused by another fellow."

Silence. He was probing.

"No," I said. I'd *liked* David stroking my hair but it hadn't *aroused* me; I know the difference.

"Or it might have crossed your mind that you'd like to try it with a fellow," he said. "See if it does turn you on."

I hadn't expected that.

"Um . . . if I had thought about it," I said, "would that mean I was gay?"

"All of us," he said, "and I'm talking about myself here as well, need to be careful about placing limits on ourselves with labels such as 'straight' and 'gay.' People are far too complex to be categorized narrowly like that. Each one of us is unique. *You're* unique! And you're not being fair to yourself if you see yourself as merely one thing or another. It's important to keep your options open, especially in regard to relationships with other people."

"Well, what if there was this bloke you liked," I said, "and he was gay, and you liked it when he touched you. Would that mean you were gay?"

"It's possible that you're placing too much emphasis on sex," he said. "Liking a person for who they are is more important than whether they're male or female, straight or gay."

"But it's important to know!" I said.

"Yes. But then, really," he said, "so what if you were?"

"You're kidding!" I said. "My dad'd kill me! He'd rip my arms off and beat me to death with them. A man's gotta be a man! He's gotta chase girls, play sports! Except for tennis. I was never allowed to play tennis. He reckons tennis is for poofs."

"Perhaps you can see how limiting *that* particular label is?" he said.

"Yeah. And with Mum it's the opposite: you gotta be *sensitive*. If you don't bawl your eyes out over soppy movies, you're *denying your feelings!*"

"It's not for anyone to tell you what you should be," he said. "Not even you at this stage of your life."

"You reckon?" I said. This was all starting to sound horribly vague.

"Over the next few years you're going to be trying out lots of ways of relating to people, both male and female, and it's important to stay open-minded. Especially about yourself."

"Um . . . yeah, but look, if I was gay, how would I know?"

"That's not a question I can answer for you," he said.

So he didn't know either. Or else he wasn't telling.

He wanted to keep on talking, but I said, "Look, thanks, you've been a great help, but I gotta go." I got out of there fast.

Try it and see? Is that what he was telling me? What a thing to tell a kid! But how else *did* you find out?

28

I drew some money out of my Building Society account and roamed around the back streets until I found a second-hand bookshop. Inside, I browsed until I'd spotted what I wanted. Then I picked out a bike magazine and a comic and brought them up to the bloke at the counter. I was the only one in the shop, so I asked, loudly, on purpose, "Do you have any of those gay men's magazines? It's my mate's birthday, I wanna give him one as a joke." So what if he'd heard the line before? He didn't know if it was for real or not this time. And he was getting paid for it.

The gay mags were on a rack behind him.

"Any one'll do," I said. "Doesn't matter." He placed one on top of my comic. "How much?" I'd drawn out twenty dollars; he charged me two.

I ran again.

Boy, was I careful crossing streets after that. Imagine getting hit by a bus with something like this in your hands! I ducked into another public toilet, locked myself in another cubicle. This one had walls daubed with three different colors of paint, a stainless steel bowl and a light bulb covered with wire mesh. The light was weaker than it had been in the first bathroom, and the smell of urine was stronger.

I was going downhill.

I sat on the bowl, my hands shaking so much I couldn't hold the magazine. I had to rest it on my knees. My fingers felt like putty, opening the cover. It was stiff and new. Only the bottom right-hand corner was creased, where someone else had done this before me, sat in the half dark with shaking fingers, perving on pictures of naked men. Or two men together.

The photography was great and they were all good-looking blokes with terrific bodies. Mostly they were naked, or they wore scraps of leather or torn singlets. There were no strategically placed potted plants. You got the lot, full on, balls and all.

I've seen this kind of stuff before. There's always a porno mag floating round at school somewhere. But it's different when you're on your own, and you don't have to stage a reaction or pretend you're not looking that hard.

There was no one watching me except the blokes on the pages. I could look for as long as I liked, and react for real.

My arms felt weak turning the pages and my knees shivered. I looked at the next and the next and the next. And yeah, I was interested. Not to the point where it got me horny. The state I was in, I don't think anything could have done that. But I got the *stirrings*, perving on naked men. I went through the whole magazine with my heart racing and my eyes getting grittier.

One of the blokes reminded me of David. He was really lean and athletic looking, and he was smiling in a "come on" sort of way. I touched his face and let my fingers creep down the page, seeing how far I could go. Seeing what it did for me.

143

So now you know.

So now I knew.

And I wished I didn't.

It was OK for them, but I didn't want it for me. I didn't want to be a poofter joke, a social outcast, a candidate for AIDS. They had each other; I was on my own.

You could die of this.

I was already dying of it. I was turning hollow inside, draining away. Slowly. Losing myself. Everything I'd thought I was, I wasn't any more.

I tried to flush the magazine down the toilet, to get rid of the evidence, but the water swirled around it and it wouldn't go past the first U-bend. Now it was soggy, and it was going to swell up and get bigger. And no way was I going to put my hand in there and pull it out, not soaked in everyone else's shit-water.

Except if I left it there, it was going to seize up the city's plumbing and I'd be to blame. It'd be all my fault, because I was gay.

I turned around and pressed my face into the corner of the cubicle, I was so ashamed. I didn't know what to do. How was I going to live with this? How was I going to hide it?

Take up body-building and make myself look macho. Go out with girls as a cover — ones who didn't want sex — there's plenty of them out there. Drop Tony. Drop photography. Become a light-house keeper. A Catholic priest. Give up everything I'd ever wanted. I couldn't have friends any more. It'd be just too risky. Because no one must know. Ever.

I couldn't bear the thought of people knowing about me. I could never let anyone get close to me again.

God, I was going to be lonely. How was I going to live

with this? How was I going to get home? How was I going to get out of this toilet even? I didn't know.

I pressed my whole body into the corner of the cubicle. *Hurt?* I hadn't known what pain was till I'd run into this. Living hurt, breathing hurt.

I wished I'd never looked. Wished I'd never lifted the lid. But the damn thing was out now, and it was crawling all over me.

29

I took up smoking on Tuesday — a pathetic attempt to commit suicide, and an excuse to talk to Vince. Everything I did was either pathetic or an excuse.

He was at the computer, typing in a program and listening to the cricket match on the radio at the same time. I asked if I could bludge a smoke and he said, "No."

I hung around anyway, rolled up my jeans and showed him the burn on my leg.

"Aw, for Chrissake, put your poor sore leg away and have one." He shoved the packet at me. "But if Mum smells it on your breath, you thieved it, OK?"

That was OK. I could steal, I could sneak, I could do anything. I stood close to the window and blew the evidence out through the flyscreen.

"Do you know if Mum's been on to Dad about the bike?" I said.

"I don't know anything about your bike." He kept his green eyes on the green screen. Vince is a master at ignoring people.

"I thought maybe she'd been at him again to get rid of it," I said. "She doesn't want me riding any more."

"There's your excuse, then. If anyone asks why you've given it up, you can say your mother made you."

"I'm not giving it up!"

"Well, I'm not talking to her for you, if that's what you want. I'm sick of trying to help you."

"I don't want you to talk to her," I said. "I'll do it myself, when she's had time to get over it. Next week. Or the week after."

"Or the week after that," he mumbled.

I must have been getting used to his snipes. They didn't hurt so much any more.

Someone hit a six at the cricket ground and Vince cheered them. He can't stand people doing things half right or half well. He only likes people who are experts, or heroes. And I've never done anything heroic in my brother's eyes.

So be a hero now!

"Um . . . David," I said. Just getting his name out was hard enough.

"What about him?" Vince's gelled spikes bristled up the back of his neck.

"Did Dad go down to see him?"

"No. No thanks to you."

"He wasn't cuddling me in the darkroom," I said.

"I know."

"Did you ask him?"

"I didn't have to. I know him, he's not interested in little boys."

146

"Thanks a lot!" I ground my cigarette into the ashtray.

"Running away again, Ace? If you hadn't taken off on your bike like you did the other day, nothing would have happened. No one would have thought anything about it. But you had to run. You're always running."

"So did David," I said. "He took off too."

"Not in a blaze of glory like you did. You make it look sus, Ace! And you made *him* look guilty."

"You weren't there. You didn't see the way she looked at us."

"Aw, who gives a stuff about the way she looked at ya?"

"I do!"

"Well, you're the only bloody one. No one else takes any notice of her."

"I had other problems that day," I said.

"You've always got problems. You're riddled with them. And I'm getting sick of them. You're always laying your shit on everyone else."

"Like who?"

"Like me! How do you think I feel about what happened? He's my mate and you made him look a creep. How do you think *he* feels? You don't know what he's been through, Ace. He didn't need that."

I didn't know what he'd been through?

"You had Mum and Dad at each other's throats. If you've got problems, do something about them. Sort yourself out."

"I did!" I said. "I phoned a telephone counselor."

"What've you got to phone a counselor about?"

"That's my business."

He saved what was on the computer. "Were you thinking of bumping yourself off?"

"Don't be stupid."

"What'd you phone about?" He took two cigarettes from the pack, lit them, and put one in the ashtray for me.

"All right, it was about girls," I said, and sat down.

"*A* girl?"

"Sort of."

"Have you got someone pregnant?"

"No."

He switched off the radio. "What's the problem?"

"This girl offered me sex the other day," I said, "and I knocked her back."

"And?"

"Blokes aren't supposed to knock girls back."

"You can if you like."

"But she's gunna spread it round now that I'm a freak, that I didn't want it, and you know how that's gunna look."

"Get in first. *You* spread it round that she's got VD."

"No!"

"Why not?"

"It's not that simple," I said.

"It's not that complicated, Ace."

He makes me feel like I'm the only person in the world who can't handle things.

"Why'd you knock her back? Any reason?"

"Yeah, because she's gross, and a sleaze-bag, and I hate her."

"Then you'd have been a jerk to take her on."

The cigarette was making my head feel gluggy, but I kept on smoking it. "There's this other girl too," I said. "Tony reckons I could have her if I wanted. It's his sister."

"Bianca?"

"No, Sophie."

"Wouldn't have thought she was your type."

"She's nice. She's got big boobs."

"If that's all you're into — who you can knock off and how big their boobs are — then you're a sleaze-bag yourself."

"No I'm not! That's the point. I don't wanna screw anyone yet. But everyone's telling me I should!"

"Everyone? Or just your over-sexed mate?"

"All the boys are the same. It's all they ever talk about — sex."

"Because they're not getting any. You can always tell the ones who are missing out, they talk the most."

"I don't wanna talk about it," I said.

"Then don't."

"And I don't wanna do it just yet either. Not with any of the girls I know at the moment, anyway."

"How about any of the blokes?"

"I know you *think* I'm gay."

"Ace, I don't think anything! Your sex drive is your own hangup. Do with it as you wish."

"Bullshit. You're the worst of the lot," I said. "You're always telling me what to do."

"I make suggestions. You don't have to listen."

"Aw sure! Everyone's on my back, telling me this, telling me that, and I know they're gunna heap ten tons of shit on me if I don't do exactly what they say."

"Stuff everyone else. Make up your own mind."

"It's not that easy."

"No, it takes guts, and you've either got them or you haven't."

"And you think I haven't."

"I think you're fartin' around looking for them."

He wants me to be like him. Like Mum wants me to be like her! And Dad wants me to be like him!

We didn't end up bosom buddies as a result of our chat, Vince and I, but for some odd reason I was glad we'd had it.

—— 30 ——

With my head still woozy from the cigarette, I went down to the darkroom and locked the door. I'd developed the negatives for David's pictures the day before. Now I threaded the strip into the enlarger and drew it along, watching frame after frame of his car beam down on to the board, then his face.

The telephoto lens had caught him, head and shoulders, looking at me, squinting slightly as if expecting something — expecting me not to take his photograph, I suppose, when I'd already done it.

I was glad now that I had, even if it had embarrassed him at the time. It gave me something to hold on to. I printed the picture and sat with it dripping in my hands. The one blond hair in his bangs glowed white and the lines running back from his eyes were trenches. I knew where he'd got them from now. I was developing similar ones myself, lying awake at night, wondering: was I or wasn't I? That business with the magazine hadn't proved a thing. Everyone looks; naked bodies of any sort are interesting, and give you a bit of a buzz.

My putting my arms around him meant more. I'd done it totally without thinking, so I figured that was more likely to be the *real* me, as opposed to the *unreal* me, the one I'd been play-acting for fifteen years. Possibly I only liked girls because everyone had told me I was supposed to. I hadn't liked Gloria.

But David was the nicest person I knew. I liked him, I liked talking to him, I liked his hand stroking my hair.

I touched my own neck, trying to bring back the feeling of his fingers there. He'd been gentle, he'd cared, and I'd never got that from any girl.

I touched his face in the photograph, the dark shadow of his jawline, his lips. And yeah, I could imagine being kissed by him. Just thinking about it made my pulse rate pick up.

I'd thought about these things before — a bit. Never in detail, though, and never with myself in the picture. But now, well . . . *What would it be like with a bloke?*

The idea of sex with girls had always frightened me. This couldn't be that much more scary. At least with a bloke you'd know what to do, having practiced on yourself.

Before, when I'd been lying in bed staring at the walls, staring at the ceiling, going round the bend, I'd thought: I might *be* it, but I'd never *do* it! But now . . . It wasn't totally out of the question. If I could hug a man, and imagine being kissed by him, why not the rest?

I didn't want to go through the rest of my life alone. I wanted to be loved and cared about like everyone else. And I didn't want to die without having done it, either. Sex is part of living, part of being close to someone. Why should I miss out?

The AIDS thing worried me, but that was going to be

151

a problem no matter who I had sex with. Knowing David, I couldn't imagine he'd be into anything other than safe sex. And, thanks to Mum, we had a houseful of condoms and pamphlets on the subject.

There'd be hassles with parents, especially with his. I was under age, and they didn't like me, but if *he* liked me, what else mattered? At least I wouldn't be alone with it any more.

Until I actually did it, I'd never really know, and I had to know. *Not knowing* was driving me insane.

And if you think I was sitting there running this through my head calmly, you're wrong. I had the hot sweats and the cold shivers, and David's photograph shook in my hands.

Wednesday was cloudy: finally, a day when you could go for a walk without being cooked. Mum went to work, Vince went to a legal studies seminar at the university, and I took to the streets.

From the opposite side of the road David's house looked deserted. The garage was closed and no one had swept the driveway for ages. It was thick with leaves.

I kept on walking. I didn't mind there being no one home. I'd made up my mind to do this, but putting it off another twenty-four hours wouldn't hurt. I felt I needed a bit more time.

I'd brought David's photographs with me to give to

him, so I took them home again. However, the idea of hanging round the house on my own, living through another day of thinking about what *I'd* say, what *he'd* say, what he'd *do!* was more than I could bear. It was there at breakfast, it went to the toilet with me. If I watched a video, it was like a voice-over in my ear. I needed a rest from it.

At Tony's house the windows were wide open and a radio tuned to ethnic music — furious mandolins — was entertaining the entire street. Tony's mother answered the door.

"You come in! You eat!" she said.

She's a nice lady, built like a margarine tub, and I like her even though she's always trying to feed me up.

"Thanks, Mrs. Martini, but I've had breakfast," I said. "Could I speak to Sophie, please?"

She called down the hallway, "Tonio!"

"No, it was Sophie I wanted to talk to."

"Oh!" She called again, "Sophia!" Then she asked, "What you have for breakfast, eh?"

"Weet-bix," I said.

She shook her head. "No good. You tell your mother: stay at home and cook your meals. A big breakfast! Lots of eggs! You too skinny. And your brother, more skinny!"

Mrs. Martini believes that "good" mothers have an obligation to turn their children into jam rolls. She's turning Tony into one. He'd better learn to do his own cooking soon or he'll end up a blimp.

He came, and was civil to me until his mother left. Then he said, "What d'you want?" He made a point of standing in the middle of the doorway like a toll booth.

"I want to talk to Sophie," I said.

"If you've come to apologize for the other day, forget it, she thinks you're a creep." Tony never was subtle. "And Gloria reckons you're a poof. She says ya kiss like one."

"That means a lot," I said, "coming from a chick who kisses like a clutch plate." I looked away, down the veranda, at the long ropy roses growing over the rails, and waited.

"Well?" Tony said.

"Well, what?"

"Are ya or aren't ya?"

Tony and I have had fall-outs before, but it's easy to make up with him. You only have to crawl a few centimeters and all is forgiven. But I didn't feel like crawling, and I didn't want the friendship back on the old basis of him knowing everything and me knowing nothing, and me having to listen to him eternally harping on about sex and wanting to compare penises. That had been fun when we were kids, but I didn't want it any more.

"You're the big authority on sex," I said. "Can't you tell straights from gays?"

The bust-up had come at the right time. We couldn't have been friends any more, anyway.

Sophie came to the door, and acted very businesslike toward me. "Yes?" she said.

"I'd like to talk to you, if you don't mind," I said.

"What about?" She made me feel like a vacuum-cleaner salesman.

"Could we talk in private?" I asked.

Tony made himself a permanent fixture against the flyscreen. *He* wasn't moving. So Sophie invited me down to the glassed-in veranda at the back of the house. I didn't feel any more relaxed down there, either. She sat upright in a wooden chair, I sank into an old lounge with collapsed springs. Mandolins twanged in the background. At least they'd screen off our conversation from the rest of the house.

"What was it you wanted?" Sophie asked.

I found myself waving my hands in circles like Tony does, but what I was saying made decent enough sense, so I was happy with that. "I just wanted you to know that what happened the other day wasn't my idea. I didn't give Gloria any reason to think I was interested. She pounced on me. I didn't encourage it."

"A girl's got a right to do what she wants," Sophie said. "Boys do! Why shouldn't a girl?"

That threw me. "I suppose you're right," I said. "I've never thought about it. It wasn't something *I* wanted, though, so I had a right to say no."

"Of course you did. Do you want me to tell her that?" she said.

"No."

"I don't see why you're telling me, then. It's got nothing to do with me."

And for a minute there I thought, *Geez, I don't know either!* Girls are so different. But I needed someone to talk to, so I kept plugging away. I showed her my poor sore leg, and she was quite sympathetic.

"Does it hurt?"

"It did at the time, when I came off the bike, but it doesn't any more."

She asked about the accident and I told her, without making myself seem *too* stupid or *too* brave. After that I steered the conversation around to photography, the one thing we had in common. I asked her about the darkroom at school because, oddly enough, I'd never

155

been in it. It didn't sound any better set up than mine.

"You can use ours any time you like," I said. "Give me a ring and let me know when you're coming, and I'll make sure it's clean."

"I don't have a camera," she said.

"I could lend you mine."

She looked ready to freak.

"You won't be interrupted," I said. "No one else in our house uses the darkroom. You'd have it all to yourself. When I'm developing pictures, I prefer to be on my own."

I was pleased I'd talked to Sophie. I didn't dislike girls. Sophie was nice, and she was interesting to talk to.

But she wasn't David.

Mrs. Minslow was unloading the dishwasher when I made my appearance in the kitchen on Friday morning. She said hello, in a tight-mouthed way. I said hello in an ordinary voice and asked if there was any bread out.

"No. It's all frozen," she said.

"That's OK," I said. "I'll toast it."

I cut up an apple for myself and poured a glass of orange juice from the fridge and waited for the toast to pop.

Apologizing to her wouldn't have bothered me. I'd

have just said, "I was having a bad day, sorry." But mentioning it would have brought up all that other stuff about David and me, and that was none of her business. I didn't want it going through her head even. So I said nothing, and neither did she, not even when I took my breakfast back to my bedroom to eat it there.

At ten, Vince went to the dentist and I took David's photographs from under my bed and set off down the road in a kind of numb state. Having covered this walk a thousand times in my head, I'd already felt everything it was possible to feel on the way. Now I was just *doing* it.

At the Rutherfords' the garage door was closed but the driveway had been swept, so I went up the path with the tree-ferns nodding over me. The gravel was quieter under my sneakers this time, and when I pressed the doorbell I heard it buzz softly somewhere inside the house.

Hello, Mrs. Rutherford.

Good morning, Mr. Rutherford.

I wasn't really looking forward to facing David's parents just yet, especially his father, and when a metallic *clunk* sounded from the garage I backed away fast. Further down the path, between the corner of the house and the garage, was a high wooden gate. I let myself through into the back yard, which was a small triangle of lawn and a huge in-ground pool. A doorway led into the back of the garage, and stepping in there was like stepping into night.

The garage was closed up and dim, except for the white strip light buzzing above the work-bench. David stood beneath it, looking at me through his hair. He didn't say a word, not even when I said, "Hi!" He hadn't shaved, and the stubble on his face made him look angry.

"I rang the front doorbell," I said.

"I didn't hear it." He went on with what he was doing. In front of him on the bench was a lawnmower with its engine stripped down. He was cleaning the bits with a toothbrush and a bowl of gasoline.

"Good thing you don't smoke," I said. With the place so closed up, you could just about taste the gas on the air.

"Yeah," he said.

He was not pleased to see me.

The sleeves of his overalls were rolled to the elbow, and his million-dollar watch sat propped up to one side of him, flashing its green numbers sixty times a minute. As I moved closer, he misted a fine spray of gasoline off the end of the toothbrush, forcing me to keep my distance.

"Got your pictures," I said, rattling the envelope.

"Thanks. It was good of you to bring them down. If you leave them over there," he said, "I'll have a look at them later." His hair wasn't gelled and it hung heavy in front of his eyes.

I could understand him being angry or embarrassed at having me turn up again. The last time we'd been together, he'd got sprung being gay — in Mrs. Minslow's eyes, anyway. And it was all my fault. He might have been hoping he'd never run into me again.

"No, ya gotta look at them *now!*" I said. "Some of them are pretty good, even if I do say so myself."

I acted chirpy, a bit childish too, bopping on the spot

like I was wired to something. It was awful being so nervous.

"I'm pushed for time at the moment," he said. "I've got this job to finish." And as he stood there, he did the poofiest thing I'd ever see him do. He flicked his hair out of his eyes by tossing his head.

"It'll only take a second," I said. "I shed blood for these pictures." I felt like I was bleeding now. What if he hated me? What if I couldn't talk him round! *It's OK to talk about last Friday!* I was trying to say. *I want to.*

He glanced at me sideways, trying to figure out why I was there, I suppose. I didn't know how to tell him. Or how else to go about this, other than to keep on bulldozing away like I was already doing, acting chirpy and cracking funnies.

"Lawnmower packed it in?" I said.

"No," he mumbled.

"Oh, I see, just practicing."

He told me what was wrong with it — a fuel blockage somewhere.

"Um . . . got another toothbrush?"

I know I take ages to make up my mind about anything, but once I do make a decision, that's it, I stick by it. And he got the message — I wasn't going away. He *had* to look at the photographs.

"Well," he held his hands out over the bowl, "I'll have to wash up first."

"That's OK!" I said. "I've got all day!" I leaned on the bench, exhausted already.

In the laundry he rubbed degreaser into his hands and washed them, then peeled off his overalls.

"Would you like a drink?" he asked.

159

"Yeah, sure." My mouth was as dry as dog biscuits.

"Coffee? Or a soft drink?"

"Coffee," I said, figuring that'd take longer to make.

It did. We went into the kitchen, and he put the pot on and walked around getting out mugs and things. I'd never seen him in "at home" clothes before and they looked like ones left over from when he was a kid. The shirt had narrow sleeves that made his arms look thin, and the jeans had been washed so many times all the blue had been wrung out of them. And they were so tight it was a wonder he could get the fly done up.

"Can I help?" I asked. Standing around doing nothing was driving me berserk.

"You can get the milk," he said.

"Where is it?"

He was standing at the sink, and I saw him lower his face and grin. "In the fridge," he said. "It's the cow's day off."

I could have cried. He was coming round, coming back to being friendly. When I opened the fridge door, my hands shook so much that all the bottles on the door shelves rattled.

He asked me if I took sugar. Only kids take sugar, it's a sign of immaturity. I said, "No." Actually, I'd never drunk coffee before either.

It was going to be a day of firsts!

The sink was gleaming, and the rest of the house gave off a noticeable silence.

"Is your mum at work?" I asked.

"Yeah. We can sit over there." He carried our mugs to a small table near a window lined with potted plants — soft ferny things, coloring the light coming in, making it cool and hazy. Our knees collided under the table as we

160

sat down, and he said, "Sorry," and moved his chair back. He wouldn't have done that before. He was still wary of me, still keeping himself under wraps.

Until I tipped the photographs out of their envelope on to the table. That changed everything.

His long eyelashes blinked. "You didn't have to do this! I only wanted *a* picture."

The photos formed a thick, glossy pile a couple of centimeters high. Of the thirty-four shots I'd taken, I'd printed twenty-seven.

"That's OK," I said. "Tell me which ones you want enlarged, and I'll blow them up for you."

The whiskers around his mouth bristled as he smiled. "This *is* large," he said.

I'd printed the lot twenty by twenty-eight centimeters: three times your standard picture postcard.

"I can do them up to this big." I showed him with my hands.

"I don't have a photo album that big." He pulled the stack toward him, grinning at *it* rather than at me. The photos were a gift, and he knew it. "This has cost you a fortune, and all I did was tune your bike for you."

"Doesn't matter," I said.

"You're going to have to let me pay you for them."

"No way! You don't even know if they're any good yet."

"Yes, I do . . . if the rest are like this."

I'd purposely put one of the best shots on the top.

He started going through them slowly, pausing over each one, handling them by the edges like you're supposed to. I got the shivers inside just watching him.

"These are really good," he said. "Excellent! Who taught you?"

161

"No one," I said. "I taught myself. Trial and error. I've been muckin' round with photography for years."

"Well, it's paid off. I would have thought they were professional." And he looked at me for the first time, I mean *really* looked, so that I was surprised all over again by the color of his eyes. We were back to being friends again, the way we'd been before.

By watching the lines come and go around his eyes I could tell which photographs he liked best, and I tried to keep a mental note of them so I could blow them up for him anyway. But my head couldn't seem to hold a thought for more than a second. It was like I was burning up energy just sitting there.

"You've got quite a talent for this," he said. "Let me know when you make your first movie, I'll be there."

"You might be in it!" I said.

He laughed. "Thanks, but I think I'd better stick to engineering."

He came to the picture I'd taken of him getting out of the car, and I said, "See? You'd make an OK movie star." It was a good shot of him, it made him look handsome, and because he wasn't smiling, it was kind of dramatic too.

He passed over it quickly. "You shouldn't have taken that one."

"Why not?"

"I don't like having my picture taken."

"Why not? You're all right. There's nothing wrong with ya. I could go for you myself."

I hadn't planned to say that. I'd had no idea *what* I was going to say, but I had planned to say something. I had condoms in my pocket, and even though I was shaking like a leaf inside, I wanted this to happen. I'd made my decision. I wanted to know once and for all what I was, so I could quit dangling over the edge of it, never sure.

Originally I'd had visions of just coming right out and telling him how I felt about him, and about what happened in the darkroom. But that was all daydreams. You can't really say things like that to people.

He just said, "You're a charmer," and passed on to the next photograph, pausing over it for a long time. It was a shot where the sun had caught the headlights and the edges of the car windows, making them gleam. "I like that one," he said. "Did you do that on purpose?"

"No," I said, "it just turned out that way."

He held it close to his face to look right into it.

Why didn't he show as much interest in me? Wasn't I cute enough? Had he forgotten what it's like not to know who you are, or what you are, or what you're supposed to do?

He insisted on paying for the pictures, and I refused. No way was I taking money off him. To change the subject, I told him about the accident. Showed him my poor sore leg and the scratches on my shoulder. Unbuttoned my shirt and flashed a bit of flesh.

Almost every other time I'd seen him, he'd touched me. Now he kept his hands on the table, or on his coffee mug. On everything but me.

"Do much damage to your bike?" he asked.

I reeled off the boring list. I didn't want to talk about bikes.

To tell the truth, I'd expected I'd only have to say something vaguely like a come-on and he'd know why I'd come and put his arm around me. And when I didn't object to that, I figured he'd get the message he could take it from there. *He* had to do it. I couldn't. I didn't know how to make advances to a man. Or to anyone else for that matter!

I wasn't going to leap on him, like Gloria had leaped on me. I had too much pride for that. Anyway, my whole reason for coming to him was that I didn't want a grope session. He was older, he'd know what he was doing. He'd be gentle. No one in my whole life had been as gentle with me as he had, and I wanted that again.

Why shouldn't I have it?

He talked about bikes. And gearboxes and Holdens. And I sat on the edge of my seat, not really listening, until I heard him say: "Well, I'd better get back to work."

He gripped the edge of the table, ready to get up. I heard his chair start to scrape the floor. He was leaving. In another second he'd be gone, and I'd never get another chance. I watched my hand shoot out and grab his.

I couldn't believe I'd done it.

I sat paralyzed. And weak. My hand, pressing his on the table, was trembling. He must have been able to feel it. I couldn't look at his face.

He had no trouble peeling my fingers away from his, and I felt my insides turn to water as he gave my hand back to me. "No," he said, really low. *No.*

My head went down and I covered my face with my hands. I wanted to die. I wanted the ground to open up and swallow me. I wanted to be obliterated so no one would ever know I'd existed, or remember anything I'd done, especially this.

Awful howling sounds started up inside me, and

even with my hands over my mouth, they came out. Whimpering sounds that burned my throat and burned my eyes. I don't know how I *didn't* die.

I felt his arm sweep around me and he pulled me to him. "Peter, I'm sorry!" he said. "I didn't mean that. I didn't mean it that way. I'm such an idiot. I'm sorry." He pulled his chair closer and put both arms around me, wrapping me up against his shoulder. "Come on, don't cry. I'm sorry. I'm sorry."

My stupid eyes leaked and my nose sniffled. I kept my face covered, and he held me for ages, rocking me and saying over and over, into my hair, "I'm sorry." He held me tight and let me cry. Like Mum used to when I'd hurt myself, or Dad even, when I was still small and hugs were OK.

"Are you all right?" he asked me eventually, and when I didn't answer, he asked again, "Hmm?"

"I dunno," I mumbled. "I just dunno."

He stroked my hair the way he had in the darkroom, letting his fingers rest along the back of my neck now and then. "What don't you know?" he asked.

"Nothin'," I said. "I don't know anything any more."

I kept my face buried against the warmth of his shoulder and the softness of his shirt; felt him breathe in slowly and ask, "Do you think you might be gay?" as if it was a question you'd ask anyone.

"I dunno," I said again.

He kept on stroking my hair. "If you're not sure, it might be an idea to find out first. You're a pretty gorgeous kid. Not too many guys'll knock you back. And you could get screwed and still not know. Is that what you want, just to get screwed?"

"No." I shook my head.

165

"No, I didn't think so," he said.

I needed a tissue, which was awful, because it meant he had to take his arms from around me and go and get one. And it wasn't the same when he came back, he couldn't just hug me again. But he sat close, with his hand on the back of my chair. I blew my nose and tried to act normal.

He asked me how old I was, and I said, "Nearly sixteen."

"You've got plenty of time. Why not wait?" he said.

"I have been waiting," I said. "I can't stand waiting. No one else is waiting!"

"I don't know about that," he said.

"All my mates are doin' it."

"Are they?" He sounded surprised.

"The girls too. All the girls are at you, and if you don't come across, they reckon you're . . ."

Oh, hell! I was acting like a kid!

"A poof?" he said.

I needed more tissues. Luckily he'd brought the whole box.

"I hope you're not planning to jump off the Gap if you are," he said.

"No! No, I wouldn't do anything like that," I said. "It'd be all right. I wouldn't mind, so long as I knew!" *And if I ended up with someone like him.* "I just gotta know!"

"I wish I could help you," he said, "but it wasn't like that for me. I think I've always known. From when I was twelve, anyway, and got an almighty crush on my swimming coach. Then it was a teacher. Then I flipped over one of the senior boys at school. There was never

166

any question about it for me. But I know it's not like that for everyone. We all do things differently. Have you been worried about it long?"

I nodded, making out I had. I know it had only been a week, but it had been a bloody long week.

He did something really nice then, he took one of my hands and held it tight between his. "Look, Peter," he said, "if I gave you the impression I was cruising you, I'm sorry. That was my fault, I should have been more careful. I like you — a lot! I think you're exceptionally cute. I just never expected you'd notice."

"I can't be *that* cute," I said. He might have been holding my hand, but he was still saying no.

"You're Vince's brother. That puts a big fullstop over you for me. Do you understand that?" *I didn't want to understand it.* "And to be totally honest with you, I think you're too young."

God, I hate being fifteen.

"How old were you?" I said, hoping to blow his argument out the window.

"I met my first lover when I was eighteen," he said. He let go my hand and sat back from me, and I wished I'd never asked. "I met him just after the HSC, which was lucky. If I'd met him the week before, I wouldn't have passed a single exam. He was beautiful. I went crazy over him. First loves are pretty special. And *he* sure was. He was also extremely possessive, and that's what finally broke us up. I wasn't allowed to talk to anyone else."

Eighteen? My turning eighteen was so far into the future, it felt like an event that might never happen. I could have cried all over again. But somehow I managed to sit there and take it *like a man*, have him touch my shoulder and tug my hair, and tell me, "You've got nothing to lose by giving yourself more time."

No, only him.

But what alternative did I have?

I could hear that rotten lawnmower calling him from the garage. "How did *you* know?" I asked, wanting to hold him there a minute longer. He understood what I meant, and he didn't mind me asking. I think I could have asked him anything.

He sipped his coffee and wet his lips and said, as if he was telling me a secret, "I just kept falling in love with men."

I'd only fallen in love with one — him — so I still wasn't sure.

"You're a sweet kid," he told me. He thanked me for the photographs, and I went home.

33

Three days later he came by the house to collect Vince, and from the family room I heard him ask for me: "Is Peter here?"

"In there," Vince told him, "expanding his mind."

I was watching the midday movie.

"Have you got your bike on the road again?" he asked, leaning on the back of one of the armchairs. I was sitting in the other. His hair was gelled, he'd shaved, and he was all dressed up again, in another immaculate white shirt with a designer label on the sleeve.

"Not yet," I said.

"Are you having trouble with it?"

"The throttle cable's broken," I said, *"and* the whole assembly."

"Can't you get it apart?"

"It *fell* apart, just about," I said, "but I can't unhook the cable from the other end."

"The carbi end?"

"Yeah."

"Can I have a look at it?"

"If you want."

He wanted to. Vince was in a hurry to go, but David said, "I know what it's like to be without wheels."

So the three of us went down to the garage, and with the few tools I had there, David worked on the cable until he'd coaxed it free. Then he showed me how to hook it up again, for when I got the new one to replace it. He gave me some clues, too, on fixing the other few things that were busted.

"There's not much you can do about these," he said, running his hand over the dents in the gas tank, and wiping the dust off at the same time. "Not that you'd want to. Dirt bikes go better with a few dings in them." He smiled. "Any mechanic will tell you that."

Beside him on the floor was an old shirt I'd been using as a rag. He picked it up and wiped his fingers on it. Vince was tapping his foot, eager to go.

"If you run into any more problems with that cable," David said, "bring the bike down. I'll have a look at it."

He hung the old shirt neatly off the end of the handle-bar, and winked at me across the gas tank as he stood up. "Any problems — you know where I am."

It was a nice offer, and I'd take him up on it if I needed help.

And maybe one day, in a couple of years' time, if I still felt the same about him, I'd turn up on his doorstep again.

Meanwhile, I had a bike to fix.

YA

Wal   Walker, Kate
             Peter

             c.1 $13.95   1/95

DUE DATE
